THE S

Mike Stott

THE STEEL TRAP

Mike Stott

This book is dedicated to my mum.

* * *

Special thanks to the following:

Mark Stretch for the invaluable work on the front cover and Jamie Long and Andrew Stafford for agreeing to be on it. Also, to my old mate Brian King.

Extra special thanks to my wife, Ellie, who will be as surprised by this as everybody else.

The Steel Trap
by
Mike Stott

To Mark

Mike Stott

Mike Stott

Introduction

Cameron could feel the blunt edge of the machete under his chin. He stood on tiptoe leaning backwards with his hands grasping at the wet edges of the sink for support.

"We were having a great night until your wee cunt of a friend told my boss to "fuck off," said the guy in the long leather coat. "Our friend is on trial. He'll go down tomorrow and we were giving him a good send off 'cos it'll be a few years before he sees the light of day again."

"I'm sorry to hear that," Cameron stammered.

"Aye, we were happy because we've just done a big deal this afternoon too. One kilo of cocaine, you know, and your friend has just spoiled it." His breath, only an inch from his victim's face, smelled of whisky and cigarettes.

"You shouldn't be telling me things like that," said Cameron. "You don't know who I am. I could be a copper."

"You'd better not be," said leather coat, jabbing the machete deeper into Cameron's chin for emphasis, his lips tight and his eyes hard.

Chapter 1

The sunlight glinted on the aircraft's wings as it taxied to a stop. Miles stood up and collected his briefcase from the overhead locker and then filed off into the terminal with the rest of the early morning business travellers on that Monday in September. He made his way to the luggage carousel and a few minutes later saw his bag of golf clubs and suit carrier come trundling towards him.

Miles exited the terminal into the airport's reception area to see Cameron standing a few yards away smiling.

"Good flight?"

"Yes, and on time too."

"Come on then, my car is in the short stay. I hope you are ready to get your English arse kicked. What did you say your handicap was again?"

"Eighteen," replied Miles.

"I thought bandits were supposed to be Mexican?" said Cameron grinning.

Miles had first met Cameron a few weeks before at a business conference in Glasgow. At the evening reception they had been introduced by one of the conference organizers.

"Do you live here?" asked Miles noting Cameron's Scottish accent.

"Aye, born and bred"

"Celtic or Rangers?"

Cameron unbuttoned his shirt cuff and rolled up his sleeve to reveal the tattoo of a lion on his arm.

Miles laughed and did the same revealing a similar tattoo with the notation around the edges "Millwall Football Club 1885."

"You're a wee hard man," laughed Cameron.

"F Troop mate," grinned Miles.

"So, what is it that you do?" asked Cameron.

"Credit Insurance. Do you know what that is?" asked Miles.

"I've heard of it, but perhaps you can enlighten me?"

"It's for businesses. It's an insurance against bad debts. Basically, most companies supply goods or services on credit. If their customer goes bust then they are out of pocket, sometimes to the extent that they go bust themselves. Credit Insurance fills that gap," said Miles.

"My business offers corporate finance and I know I few people who would be interested in that," said Cameron. "You really need to speak to my Dad though, he's the Managing Director. When is the next time you are up in Glasgow?"

Miles was very rarely in Glasgow. In fact, he was very rarely outside of London. He wasn't even a salesman. He used to be, but now he dealt with claims. On the other hand, everybody in his company had a new business target and if it wasn't met it always impacted seriously on your end of year bonus. Sensing an opportunity to solve that problem for the foreseeable future a date was set for a meeting with Cameron's father.

"Do you play golf?" asked Cameron

Miles nodded

"Come up the day before then and bring your clubs."

In the September sunshine Dalhanny Golf Club was everything Miles had expected a 150-year-old Scottish links course to be. As his final putt rolled in on the 18th green he smiled and shook Miles's hand.
"That's 30 quid you owe me Sassenach," grinned Cameron. "Come on, let's go to the bar, it's not too late for lunch."

Cameron's car pulled up outside the Ritz Hotel in the city centre. Miles got out already feeling the effects of three pints of heavy.
"I'll drop the car back home and see you back here at 6.30." said Cameron. "Don't forget you owe me 30 quid!"
"Fuck off, you'll get your money," laughed Miles already comfortable with his new friend.

By 11pm the town had been well and truly hit by the two new friends. Drinks in the hotel continued to a meal in a smart restaurant, some more drinks and then eventually ending up back in the sophisticated bar of the Ritz.
With both men friendly and outgoing it didn't take too long to start talking to the bar's other late-night inhabitants. At first they talked to the TV comedian who had just finished a stand-up gig over the road in the Playhouse, but it seemed that anything amusing he had to say stopped as soon as he walked off stage.
Miles and Cameron then started to talk to two Scottish guys, both engineers, who were working in Glasgow and staying at the hotel. They introduced themselves as Gary and Paul. As the conversation developed it transpired that both had served in the Falklands War. As an enthusiast of military history Miles was keen to

learn more and the four stood in a group chatting, nodding and smiling.

Unexpectedly, the group was joined by a fifth man. He stood with a pint in his hand listening to the conversation but saying nothing. After a few questioning glances Gary piped up "Can I help you pal?"

The man looked sweaty and wide eyed, clearly drunk or stoned or both. "I'm just waiting fur mae friends. You dinnae mind if I stand here do you?" Everybody shrugged, nodded their heads and continued their conversation.

A few minutes later a man entered the bar in a leather trench coat, which reached to his ankles. Miles wondered briefly why he was wearing such a big coat when it was so warm. He then noticed that the stranger had peeled off the group to join the man in the leather coat and two other men who had just wandered in.

"Did you not think that was rude?" said Gary to Miles. "He just sidled up to us, nothing to say and then fucks off."

"He's just drunk," said Miles.

"No, I'm not having that. I'm going to have a word," said the Gary.

Miles watched as Gary confronted the group but after a few seconds his accusatory finger stabbing ceased abruptly, he stopped speaking and appeared to cower slightly. The engineer returned to Miles's group clearly perturbed.

"I'm away to my bed. I don't like the clientele," he said as he swept past.

The evening wore on with more drink being taken until Miles and Cameron were very drunk with their friend, Paul, being not far behind them. At around 12.30 the bell rang for last orders. Despite being sufficiently refreshed and with nearly full pints Miles motioned to the others that he should get another round.

"Dinnae worry about that," said the Paul, "last orders is for people not staying here. There's nae hurry,. Cheers."

At that moment the silent stranger once again appeared on the edge of the group. "We're nae residents here but you will nae tell will ya?" he asked.

"Fuck off, you're fine," said Miles filled with pints of bonhomie.

The strangers face froze and stared stonily back at Miles. "Did you just tell me to fuck off?"

"No, no, I meant you're okay," said Miles attempting to calm matters with a wink.

"Oh. I thought you told me to fuck off," said the stranger coldly and turned to re-join his cohort. Miles shrugged and took another sip of his pint.

Drunk and tired the three companions now took a seat at the bar. Cameron pushed back his barstool and weaved towards the men's' toilets. Miles continued chatting amiably with the Scottish engineer when he noticed Cameron exiting the toilet far more quickly and with more purpose than when he entered it. He looked pale. "Everything alright mate?" asked Miles.

"No," said Cameron shaking his head. "No"

Miles raised his eyebrows questioningly. "You have just told the biggest gangster in Glasgow to fuck off," said Cameron slowly. "His mate, in the leather coat followed me in. He pulled a machete on me. You have seriously pissed them off."

"It's all a mistake, I will go and apologise" said Miles pushing back his barstool.

"No," said Cameron, pushing him back in his seat. "Stay here. We must wait until they leave. You are safe here but don't go to the toilet or anything."

"Aye, if he wants you he'll have to go through me" said Paul.

"This is ridiculous" said Miles and filled with the bravado of two gallons of beer crossed to the hotel reception desk. "Can you call the police please? My friend has just been threatened in the toilet with a machete."

"You've done what?" said Cameron looking shocked and shaking his head. "You don't report these people to the police."

"I'm not scared of them. I'm Millwall," slurred Miles.

"Listen pal," said Cameron grabbing Miles's arm, "this is serious. These people are serious. That's Jaimie McGovern over there and you told him to fuck off"

"No, I didn't, he just misunderstood," protested Miles. "Who is he anyway?"

"He runs all the drugs in Glasgow. He took over from Fatboy Wilson."

"Who's Fatboy Wilson?" said Miles.

"He used to run all the rackets in Glasgow, but he was shot on his way home. Nobody knew who did it but McGovern took over. Listen Miles, I have to live in this town. I can't be here when the police come. I'm going to slip out and go home.

Cameron looked across the bar nervously and started to stand up. " I will pick you up tomorrow at 9.30 okay?

My advice is to tell the police that you made a mistake. You misheard me, there was no machete okay? Don't mention my name, I'm just a guy you were talking to at the bar. See you tomorrow. Be careful." At this Cameron glanced at McGovern's crew and slipped away towards the exit.

Two police officers arrived and made their way to the hotel reception desk. Miles saw that the McGovern crew had registered this and immediately got up and left. Paul tapped his hand "I'm away to my bed. Good to meet you."

The police officers approached Miles and took him into a side room. The interview lasted less than 15 minutes. Miles couldn't mention Cameron by name and so all he had to say was that the stranger he was drinking with had said he was threatened in the toilets.

"With a machete?" asked the police officer.

"Possibly, although I might have misheard," said Miles.

"And where is your friend now?" asked the police officer.

"He left."

"And the man who threatened him?"

"He left when you came in."

The police office pulled a sour face. Another drunk businessman wasting her time.

"I suggest we leave it there sir?"

Miles nodded.

Chapter 2

Miles woke with a raging thirst. He looked at the clock on the table next to the bed. It was 9.12. He stumbled to the bathroom and hastily filled two tumblers of cold water from the sink draining both in one glug. He then turned and noisily vomited into the toilet.

He was just flushing the toilet for the second time when he heard a knock at his door. Dressed only in his boxers he opened it by an inch and peeped through. "Who is it?" he asked blinking.

"Miles, it's Gary and Paul from last night, said Paul.

"Oh hi," said Miles opening the door a couple of inches wider.

"Listen pal, sorry to disturb you, but we have just been down for breakfast and they are all over the hotel looking for you - McGovern and his boys from last night and a few more by the looks of it. They asked if I had seen you, but I said you had already left," continued Paul. "If I were you I would stay up here for a while."

"Okay, thanks," said Miles suddenly very alert. The room telephone began to ring.

"Listen guys I have to get that but thanks," said Miles.

"Good luck be careful" said Paul.

"Aye, be careful," said Gary as they both turned away.

Miles closed the door and grabbed the handset from the receiver.

"Miles, it's Cameron. I'm in Reception. They are all over the hotel looking for you."

"I know, I heard," said Miles noticing a shake in his voice.

"Stay in your room. I have asked the manager to come up and sort out your bill and he will take you out the back way. I'll be outside in my car," said Cameron.

Miles took less than five minutes to shower, get dressed and pack. He was just putting his tie on when there was a knock at the door. "Who is it," he called through the door.

"Mr. Dixon, it's the manager. I have been asked to come up and settle your bill."

Miles opened the door.

"There was some unpleasantness last night I understand?" the manager smiled apologetically. "I have brought your bill and the credit card machine."

Once the transaction was processed Miles followed the manger to a service lift, which took them down to the hotel kitchens on the ground floor. The manager led the way to the kitchen entrance, which exited onto the back yard of the hotel where deliveries were usually made. Cameron sat parked in a white Hyundai SUV.

Miles thanked the manager and made his way to the Hyundai. He opened the back door and threw his suit carrier into the back seat.

"Got my clubs?" he asked Cameron as he climbed into the front seat.

"Yes, they're in the back but what are you doing?" barked Cameron. "Get in the back seat and put that blanket over you. Those guys are all over the place." Miles did as he was told.

Miles and Cameron sat at a back table in a café on the Pollokshaws Road nursing mugs of tea and taking small bites at the bacon sandwiches they had ordered.

"Listen Miles, I am sorry for running out on you last night," said Cameron "but these are heavy, heavy people. I think what happened in the hotel this morning demonstrates what we were up against." He stirred his tea.

"What you did is enough to get you stabbed or slashed. I have to live in this town. Fortunately, I wasn't the one who told McGovern to fuck off. They let me leave the hotel last night no bother but by calling the police you just stirred that wasps' nest up even more.

Cameron looked at his watch. "We're seeing my dad at 12 and then I suggest that I get you back to the airport and out of harms' way," he smiled.

"Listen, I'm sorry but you know I didn't mean to do this. What I said wasn't meant as an insult," said Miles.

"I know," said Cameron. "We were just in the wrong place at the wrong time. These guys are nutters. A guy accidently trod on McGovern's foot in a bar last year and he was found outside later half beaten to death with a snooker cue. The guy refused to say anything to the police, but everybody knew what happened."

"And you say he took over from a guy called Fatman?" asked Miles.

"Fatboy Wilson," Cameron corrected. "It's a whole dynasty. My dad has told me about it. The Italians originally started the protection rackets in this city before the war. They did other stuff too: in the docks, prostitution, stuff like that. Come the war though and they were all interned as potential enemy agents on the Isle of Man. This left the way open for the local firms to take over." He paused to sip his tea.

"Glasgow was very heavily bombed in the war and these guys would join up as ARP wardens and loot the bomb sites. All sorts of things were looted: money, jewellery, furs and they were all fenced through the local markets. They also started forging ration cards and petrol coupons. By the time the Italians were released the Glasgow gangs were so strong that they couldn't get back in the game.

"When rationing stopped in the '50s they had to rely more on their protection business. This is where Arthur J. Wilson came along, Fatboy's dad. At first, he was just a heavy, breaking arms to get paid. By the '60s, however, he had come up with a couple of other ways to make money." Miles raised his eyebrows in question.

"He owned a couple of nightclubs, Cameron continued, "and he noticed that the kids, particularly the mods, were taking speed. Looking into this he found that a lot of this was US Airforce surplus.

"The yanks had manufactured amphetamine sulphate to keep their bomber crews awake. The RAF did too but quaintly they called them "wakey, wakey" pills. At the end of the war a lot of it was destroyed but some simply sat around in crates in military warehouses. Nobody ever checked these crates and it was pretty easy to siphon it off with a bent warehouseman simply saying the goods had perished.

"There was only so much military surplus though and stocks were beginning to run out because other gangs had latched on to the scam. Arthur then got lucky." Cameron looked up to check the clock on the wall of the café.

"One of his men was leaning on a Russian guy who had a tailor's shop in the West End. How he got there I don't know but it turned out that he had been in the Red Army, which liberated Berlin. The guy couldn't pay his debt but in return for being forgiven it he showed Arthur a recipe for speed that was in a Russian Army field manual. It turned out that Joe Stalin was handing out speed to his soldiers and this stuff could be manufactured in the field using basic chemicals.

"Arthur set up a lab and cornered the market in Glasgow and supplied other gangs too. That was his start in drugs but by the 1980s the whole thing had moved on, mainly to cocaine, and he was hooking up with the Italian mafia to bring it in and he would distribute it. This is where Fatboy got involved. He had been brought up to take over from his dad."

"In the '60s Arthur also noticed that the Krays in London had started a Long Firm racket" continued Cameron.

"Yes, I know about those. I was taught about them when I started in Credit Insurance," Miles butted in. "You open up a firm dealing in goods that can be easily sold. In the '60s it was fridges and TVs. The firm places small orders with suppliers at first and begin to establish a line of credit, paying on time and supplying fake references from other companies that they control. At the end large orders are placed, the goods are sold at a discount or moved on to another crooked firm and the business is wound up leaving all the suppliers with large bad debts that they can't collect." Cameron blinked, acknowledging his agreement.

"With the insolvency laws it is hard to prove that a crime has been committed," Miles continued. "The Directors of the firm are usually patsies so if they get struck off, which hardly ever happens, it doesn't matter. I still get claims come across my desk like this from time to time. They have to be a bit more sophisticated now though or they are too easy to pick up."

Cameron nodded, "Yes, that's one way. There are a couple of others. Have you seen the film "Goodfellas"?"

Miles nodded.

"Well one of Arthur's favourite tricks was the same as in the film. He would find a local businessman who is doing well for himself. It's not that difficult in Glasgow. Who's got a new Porsche, who's moved to Hillhead that sort of thing. And then Arthur walks through the door and offers to be his partner. The guy is usually creditworthy so Arthur encourages him to order more goods and then at the optimum moment the business goes bust. Those who say no get their premises burnt down, if they are lucky, and those who say yes end up without a business. He drove a couple of guys to suicide doing this.

It was this way that Arthur got into the Steel Stockholding business," Cameron continued. He found a guy with a yard and a warehouse and a few trucks but instead of pulling the long firm stunt on this one he turned it into a legitimate business, well legitimate for him. It's called Thistle Steel. It's owned by McGovern now, he took over all of Arthur's operations when Fatboy got shot."

"Why would they want to go into steel stockholding?" asked Miles.

"Because he needed to have a legitimate front," answered Cameron.

"You can't be living in a huge house and driving flash cars without being able to account for it in some way. Remember they got Al Capone eventually for tax fraud not racketeering? Thistle Steel gives him an opportunity to clean his drugs money. Since Arthur got involved it has become a big player in the steel sector, it's probably the fourth or fifth largest stockholder in the UK, although Arthur could never keep his hands out of the till and very nearly came a cropper for it."

Miles raised his eyebrows questioningly.

"If you give these types of guys a choice that they could make the same amount of money by doing things legitimately or by breaking the law most of them will always take the latter. It's not about the money. It gives them a buzz. It's sticking two fingers up to the Establishment. It's their fatal flaw if you like.

"Back in the '80s he set up this scam. Arthur, like most stockholders at the time, bought a lot of his stuff from British Steel. Now there are different qualities of steel, grade A being the best and grade C the worst. Arthur either leant on or bribed the guy who's job it was to grade the steel to sell him grade A steel but to make it look like it was grade C, so it was considerably cheaper. Arthur then sold it to his customers as premium quality steel, which it was.

"Arthur was able to undercut the market, but legitimate companies were wary of dealing with someone like Arthur, so he also supplied to people who couldn't get credit anywhere else, the deal being that if you couldn't pay, he would break your legs and take your stock, or worse." Miles shook his head in disgust.

"He had a guy, a former Commonwealth Middleweight Champion, who would collect the debts on his behalf. This guy had some reputation when it came to collecting debts. I heard he once held a guy who owed money over a vat of pickling acid until he agreed to pay. It might have been true, it might not have been, but Arthur was always happy to let these stories get out. It burnished his reputation as a hard man and made getting paid easier.

15

"The problem came when British Steel had their books audited. It was by one of the big firms of accountants. They spotted that there was a hole in the numbers and traced it back to large quantities of grade A steel being sold at grade C prices to Arthur. The police were called and the guy on the inside confessed to everything. Arthur was arrested the next day and for all the world it looked like his number was up.

"It took a while for the trial to come to the Crown Court, but the evidence looked rock solid. The prosecution had done a deal with the guy on the inside to turn Queens Evidence and the police had put him and his family in a witness protection programme."

Cameron looked around the café to check that nobody was listening to their conversation. He lowered his voice.

"Then, just before proceeding were due to start, it was announced that the Attorney General had passed a resolution that he was too ill to stand trial. It was said that Arthur had cancer and was on his deathbed.

"Apparently, the resolution didn't let him off though. He could be called to answer the charges in the future but he never did. He lived for another 25 years and when he died some journalists investigating the story for his obituary found that any records relating to the charges had been destroyed years before. A few other minions at Thistle Steel were sent down but Arthur got them good lawyers and most got off on appeal or, if not, they were looked after when they got out"

"How did he manage to pull that one off?" asked Miles.

Cameron shrugged. "Nobody knows. It could be intimidation of somebody at the Attorney General's office. If someone threatened your kids what would you do? Or it could be blackmail. You get people to investigate someone's background and find a dirty secret that would ruin them if it ever saw the light of day. Or straight bribery, but that's a pretty blunt instrument and unlikely to work in circumstances like this. Of course, I have my own theory," said Cameron with a glint in his eye.

"Which is?" said Miles leaning his head to one side.

"You have to understand about Glasgow," said Cameron. "It isn't like other cities. For a start, there's a massive religious divide. On the one side you have the Catholics who support Celtic and think that they are Irish. On the other side you have the Prots who support Rangers and are Loyalists to a man. You've seen the Orange Marches in Belfast, Prince Billy, the Battle of the Boyne and all that?"

Miles nodded.

"Same here," said Cameron. "And like Belfast it's traditionally the Prots that run everything and the Catholics get excluded. It was decades before a Catholic ever played for Rangers. Mo Johnston, remember him and all the fuss in the newspapers about it?"

Cameron's voice dropped to a whisper. "The thing that underpins this dominance though seems to be the Masons. You must be a Prod to be in the Masons and the members aren't just local shopkeepers, they are senior policemen, judges, magistrates. Very useful people to know."

Cameron looked around again to check that nobody was listening. "Glasgow has the oldest and probably most influential lodge anywhere. I don't know if Arthur was a member, but he had a box at Rangers. If not, I bet his briefs were. We all know that they can ask favours of each other and that none of them can refuse. I am sure some big favours get asked and that some of them are granted," Cameron smiled.

"So, McGovern runs it all now though?" said Miles. "How did that happen? Did he move in after Fatboy was killed?"

"No, no," Cameron shook his head. "McGovern was Fatboy's friend. He was his minder. Fatboy wasn't like his dad. He wasn't brought up in the Gorbals and fights in the Barrowlands every Saturday night. No, it was Fettes College for the wee lamb. As his name suggests, he grew up fat and weak." Cameron pulled a face, pretending to be fat and stupid"

"When he came into the business Arthur didn't know what to do with him. Then one night a fight broke out at one of his clubs. One guy took on three sailors who were on leave and he was the only one left standing at the end of it. That guy was Jaimie McGovern. Arthur took on McGovern as muscle, but it turned out that the lad was not just a vicious psychopath, he had brains too.

"In a way McGovern was the son that Fatboy never was. He trained the kid up in all aspects of his operations and made sure he kept an eye on Arthur Junior. Arthur then had a stroke and was paralysed down one side so Fatboy took over and was running the operation into the ground. Sensing his weakness other gangs had moved into Arthur's territory. There was a turf war and Fatboy was losing." Cameron looked nervously around and leaned across the table so that only Miles could hear.

"Then he got killed. It was one Sunday morning, he was just walking down for the newspapers. A drive by with a shotgun. Arthur died the following week and

McGovern made Mrs. Wilson an offer that she couldn't refuse to take over the whole operation."

"How do you know all of this?" asked Miles

"In Glasgow these guys are like celebrities. They are vicious bastards, but some people will always see them as being Robin Hood. You hear a lot of stories in the pubs and clubs, but the local press are all over them too. It's Glasgow's version of Coronation Street." Cameron looked at his watch. "We had better go."

"Okay. What happened to the guy who turned Queens Evidence though?" asked Cameron.

"He was found hanging in a wood a few months later. The Coroner said suicide. He might have been right. You wouldn't want those bastards on you case."

The meeting with Cameron's father was brief and perfunctory. After the events of the previous night and the hangover beginning to kick in Miles was keen to conclude matters. Vague promises were made to work together but within an hour he was gratefully walking through the Departures lounge of Glasgow airport. He made a call to Kath.

"Hello sweetheart, I'm at the airport. I should be back home about 6ish...Yes, fine. Yes, a good night out. Pretty uneventful. How's Evie?"

It was with a sense of relief that Miles took one last look at Glasgow before the plane climbed above the bank of grey clouds. I shan't be coming back here in a hurry he thought. Not even if Millwall get Celtic in the European Cup he smiled to himself.

Chapter 3

Jaimie McGovern's fist smashed into the soft target. He grunted. Sweat dripped from his face and onto his wet vest.

"Okay, that's enough," said Wes letting go of the punchbag. "You can cool down with a bit of cycling for ten minutes and then go and get showered. See you again tomorrow."

Jaimie looked around the gym. Running machines and stationery bicycles stood in long rows. Banks of weight training machines stood in one corner. The mid-morning sun shone through the windows making the chrome equipment glint. An Eminem track was playing over the sound system. He felt good.

Jaimie trained every day, sometimes twice. In a year he had shed twenty pounds and had replaced most of the clothes in his wardrobe. All his suits had had to be recut with two inches taken off the waist of his trousers and the jackets widened to accommodate his bulging shoulders and neck.

It hadn't always been this way, he thought. Since the day that he was born Jaimie McGovern's existence had teetered on the brink of catastrophe. He did not remember his parents. He was born in 1972 in Glasgow Royal Maternity Hospital to a junkie mother and a father who had disappeared probably on the day that he was conceived. Years later when he had ordered a Birth Certificate in order to apply for his first Passport, he noticed that the box corresponding to Name of Father was marked "unknown."

He did not know why his mother had continued with the pregnancy but maybe it was to get on the priority list for a council flat? Jaimie learned later that he had lived with his mother for the first two years of his life in the Red Road flats in the North End of Glasgow. He still had occasion to visit his first home even today. Eight hideous 31-storey towers. Monuments of modernist misery; plagued by rats and cockroaches: of the standard kind and of the human variety.

Each block was a vast labyrinth of crime, alcoholism and drug taking, each floor representing its own special corner of hell. Jaimie's visits these days were always to sort out some problem with his drugs business: to collect a late payment from a pusher or to resolve an issue over territory. He hated the corridors covered in graffiti, dried vomit and excrement and the crunch of broken glass under his shoes. His nose wrinkled in the lifts and stairwells that reeked of piss and damp. He always had the suit he was wearing dry cleaned after each reluctant expedition to the rotting dreams of the deluded architects and town planners of the 1960s.

At the age of 26 months, Jaimie had been taken into care by the local council. The report by the social worker was the inevitable tale of neglect, malnourishment and violence. His first memories were of the Children's Home in which Social Services placed him: the dormitory with the tall windows and the ever-present smell of carbolic soap. He remembered the gentle sound of crying from the other boys every night, particularly the new ones, but he never cried himself.

For a few years he had been a happy boy. He went to the local school and played in the grounds of the home with the other boys. He was even happy to eat the food, which many of the other children were revolted by. He greedily ate their leftover white sauce and carrots and tapioca pudding, which the other kids called frogspawn. He even accepted being punished with a slipper and later, as he got older, a cane. This was his reality: he could not envisage a different life.

He was eleven or twelve years old when the abuse started. Mr. Bennett and his wife ran the home. They lived in a little bungalow by the main building and were assisted by women the children called nurses who came in during the day. On Sunday afternoons after lunch the kids would all gather in the television room. There was usually an old film on: Zulu or the Dambusters, Jaimie remembered. It was always then that Mr. Bennett appeared. The home was quiet on a Sunday. It was the nurses' day off and Mrs. Bennett always retired to the bungalow for a few hours respite before putting the girls to bed.

Jaimie was always afraid of Mr. Bennett. The older boys called him "Bender." Bender Bennett. He did not know why. Maybe it was the way the cane bent as he swished it down onto your bare bum? Or perhaps it was the way he insisted that a boy bent over his desk before inflicting the punishment?

On those quiet afternoons Mr. Bennett would always select a boy and take him to his office. He did not know what happened there, but the boys always returned to the television room and sat silently watching the screen for the rest of the day.

Only once had a boy returned crying. He was called Colin. He picked up a vase and threw it at the television. Mr. Bennett had carried the hysterical boy away and caned him. Soon after Colin had tried to run away. When they caught him, they moved him to another home and Jaimie had never seen him again.

Sunday afternoons had been a peaceful sanctuary for Jaimie. The food at lunchtime was always better: roast beef, Yorkshire puddings and roast potatoes. He would sit on the battered sofa in the television room entranced by films where the men spoke with clipped English accents and not the Scottish burr he was used to. When Mr. Bennett selected him to visit his office he took away any sanctuary or peace forever.

Jaimie joined the boys who returned silently to the television room with glazed eyes. What Bender Bennett did to him was unspeakable. Literally so. All the boys who were his victims never gave words to their experiences. They were frightened and ashamed but worse, they were isolated. Jaimie was not chosen every week and he learned to be absent from the television room when Mr. Bennett came calling. He soon realised though that if Bender had a desire for a particular boy then there was nowhere to hide.

Jaimie thought about the man who visited the Home to take them for football. The way he would look down the front of their shorts to make sure that they were not wearing underpants and how he would block the exit from the shower while he observed the naked boys. Then there was the man at Cub Scouts who groped you when nobody else was looking. Were all men like this? It seemed so.

When Bender had finished, he always told the boys not to say anything. "No one will believe you and you will be sent away, like Colin," he warned them. He would give them a pound "for sweets." Then he would hold his office door open. "Now fuck off," he would growl. After that first encounter Jaimie never ate sweets again but some of the boys would eat bags full trying to fill a void that would always gape open.

Jaimie's behaviour changed almost overnight. He would shoplift from the local newsagent and fight with the other boys. His schoolwork suffered too. He was regularly being sent out of class for disruptive behaviour. One day having been sent out of a lesson he wandered along to the school hall instead of standing outside the classroom, as he was supposed to.

The wooden climbing frame had been arranged for the forthcoming games lesson and four long ropes hung from the ceiling. Jaimie took the lighter that he had stolen from his pocket. He held it to the end of one of the ropes and watched in a satisfied way as the dry fibres began to smoulder and then to flame. The fire had reached halfway up the rope before the smoke alarm began to shriek and the ceiling had begun to blacken and burn before his astonished teacher came into the hall.

Jaimie was excited when the fire alarm started ringing and the whole school was evacuated. The three fire engines that arrived were for something he had done. He smiled.

Jaimie never went back to the Children's Home. After questioning him at the station the police took him to a special secure centre for young people. He was pleased. A few weeks later he appeared before a Youth Court and it was decided that he should remain at the Centre until he was 16. He had escaped from Bender Bennett.

The boys at the Centre were different from the ones at the Home. They were damaged but in a different way. He noticed that if they were hurt, they would not retreat into themselves. Instead, they would swear, they would break things and they would fight. Violence became a way to solve problems and to feel in control.

Whatever, retribution the authorities chose to inflict on him did not matter to Jaimie. He had been locked up for the whole of his life. Besides, nobody had done anything to protect him. When he told the police about Bender they had laughed. It was almost as if all these men belonged to some secret club. No, it was down to him to protect himself.

He fought regularly about almost anything: if someone took too long on the bog, if someone was English, anything. Quite often, he got badly hurt but he did not care. He realised quickly that he could not remember the pain inflicted on him during fights. Physical damage was nothing. Physical damaged healed.

At night his thoughts turned to violent fantasies. As soon as he was out, he would return to the Home and he would carve Bender up, slowly, inflicting the most pain possible. When they asked him why he would tell them. Let them laugh at him then.

Jaimie's acts of violence against other inmates of the Centre and the warders meant that he was a frequent visitor to the Youth Court. By increments years were added to his previous sentence. He became the longest standing inmate and the hardest. Every racket ran through him.

At the age of nineteen he was eventually released. He had nowhere to go and checked into a hostel that the Centre had arranged for him.

The next morning, he went to visit Jimmy, a former inmate of the Centre who had been released a few weeks early. He had promised to get Jaimie a combat knife. It was ready for him when he arrived. He took the oiled weapon from its sheath and inspected the hooked blade and the serrated teeth. He gingerly touched the edge. It was sharp enough to shave with. It exactly matched his requirements.

The following day, Jaimie stood hidden beside the tool shed in the grounds of the Children's Home. He watched the comings and goings from the main building and from the bungalow for several hours. He had not seen Bennett.

After a while he remembered that Bender drove a green Mini Metro. He looked around the car park but there was no car like that. It then occurred to him that it had been six years since he was last here. Maybe Bennett had got another job or retired? After waiting a few more minutes he walked to the main building and entered. The secretary's office was still there but he did not recognise the woman sitting behind the electric typewriter.

"Can I help you?" she asked.

"I'm here to see Mr. Bennett."

The woman looked surprised. "That won't be possible. I'm afraid he's dead." She took Jaimie's disappointed look as one of remorse and continued: "Yes, two years ago. His wife went to wake him up one morning and found him dead. It was a massive heart attack. He died in his sleep thankfully. Were you a friend of his?"

Jaimie shook his head and turned away. As he walked up the drive his mind was racing. His fists were clenched in fury. Bender died peacefully in his sleep not choking on his own blood on the floor of a car park with his entrails hanging out. It was an ending that he did not deserve. He had inflicted years of misery on generations of innocent children and walked away scott-free. The lucky bastard.

Chapter 4

There were two ways into the world of Insurance and Finance in the City of London. The first way was through Public School and university and the second way was through the East End. Miles Dixon fell into the second category. Well almost.

Miles had been born and brought up in Peckham Rye rather than the traditional recruitment grounds of Barking, Bow and Bethnal Green. His mum, his dad and his brother, Charlie, had lived on the Peabody Estate opposite the Rye, a welcome stretch of parkland in the concrete jungle of South East London.

Miles's dad, Harry, was a butcher at Smithfield market and left the flat at 2a.m most mornings so in his memory he was either out or asleep. His mum kept strange hours too, but at the other end of the day. She was a cleaner and worked for the credit insurance underwriter, Surety and Guarantee, on Fenchurch Street in the City.

In his formative years Miles pursued his twin hobbies of boxing in a club on the Old Kent Road and watching Millwall at the Den on Saturday afternoons

Miles was bright but the school he went to was crap. It was less like a Comprehensive School and more like a prison. Bullying and intimidation were a regular thing and although Miles could box it wasn't much good against three guys two years older than you who wanted your dinner money.

He had tried to fight back once but had found that street fights weren't like boxing matches. Trapped in a headlock as a fist swung in his face he had ended up with lips the size of Mick Jagger's for a week. In the medical room he told the teacher that someone had kicked a football in his face by accident.

"You should have grabbed him by the balls son," was all his dad said when he got home although his mum had cried and threatened to go and see the Headmaster. "Don't be so stupid, Sharon," said his dad. "What do you think they will do to him then?"

At first, he went hungry all day and then he stopped carrying money and brought in sandwiches, which he said he had spat on if the bullies wanted them. It didn't stop them been chucked on the floor and stamped on from time to time though.

As he grew older and larger the intimidation eventually stopped. One Saturday on the way to watch Millwall he ran into Max who he knew from the boxing club. At 18 Max was 3 years older than Miles. "Come for a drink," said Max and Miles had found himself standing in the Green Man pub with half a dozen men all aged between 18 and 25. They were friendly, and Miles found a pint of beer being put in his hand and then another.

He walked with them to the Den. They laughed at the guy handing at kidney donor cards to the travelling Birmingham fans. They went through a different turnstile than Miles normally would and stood together at the back joined by twenty or so others. As the Birmingham fans began to sing Miles saw the faces of his compatriots turn towards them, their arms raised, their fingers pointed. "F Troop. F Troop," they chanted.

Miles loved being part of F Troop. They were the Praetorian Guard of the Millwall fans. The elite. The hard men. They treated him like a brother and everybody at school, in the street and in the pub either gave him a wide berth or treated him like a long lost relative. He got a Millwall tattoo with the money for his 16th birthday and then hid it under long sleeved shirts from his mother for a month. "You silly sod," she said when she saw it and clipped him round the ear. "Who's going to give you a job with that bloody thing?" His dad just laughed when he found out.

At school the lessons continued to be controlled riots and Miles learnt nothing. Come the summer Miles had passed three exams: An O Level in English, because he could already speak that, another in English Literature and the third one in Maths. Numbers had always come easily to Miles. He had a party trick that he could answer any sum given to him quicker than you could do it on a calculator.

It was mid-August. The beginning of a new football season and Millwall were playing their local rivals West Ham at home. Miles had arranged to meet Max and the rest of F Troop at the Green Man. On the way to the ground Miles could feel that the atmosphere was a lot more charged than usual with a significant police presence. Groups of opposing fans chanted and hurled abuse at each other as the police on foot and on horses attempted to keep them apart. Millwall won 1-0 although nobody in F Troop took very much notice of the game, their attention fixed on the away end full of West Ham supporters.

After the game F Troop walked back to the Green Man still unable to get near their rivals. At about 7.30 Harry the Dog, one of the older members of F Troop rushed into the pub. "There's 10 of them walking down Coldblow Lane, bold as brass!" he shouted. Miles and his new friends spilled into the street and the chant went up "F Troop."

The police had gone, and the place was deserted. The West Ham fans turned to see their rivals 50 yards away running towards them. Miles was in the middle of the chasing pack with Max. It was hot and with most of the pursuers having consumed nearly a gallon of beer the West Ham fans were getting away. It seemed that this would be a chase for nothing, as usual. As they rounded a corner they saw that one of them had stopped, he looked back and started trying to run again but he was limping badly.

The first F Troop boot kicked at his leg followed by a punch to the back of his head. The kid fell and then looked up at his attackers. He was about 15 and he was crying. Crawling and trying to get up his body was rained by flying kicks and stamps. He curled up into a foetal position but still the attack didn't stop.

Miles stood and watched as they took the boy apart. He remembered watching a documentary on TV which said if you stumbled upon a bear in Canada that if you curled up it would usually stop attacking you. These men didn't. They continued to punch and kick the limp form as if excising retribution for all the hurt they had ever felt, for all their frustration and disappointment. He looked at Max who was grinning. Miles felt sick.

At the boxing club the following Wednesday Mick, the trainer, called Miles and Max together to do some sparring in the ring. The pair had not spoken since the events of the weekend. Max, who was a few inches taller than Miles, grinned down as they touched gloves as a sign for the sparring to begin.

Miles danced backwards as Max came forward and delivered a right cross. Miles bobbed down as the punch flew over his head and then moved to his left and threw a hard, low punch under his opponent's guard connecting just below his right ribs where his liver was. Max gasped and bent at the waist his arms up to protect his trunk. Miles moved back a step, straightened up and smashed a hard-left hook which connected heavily with his adversary's headguard. He watched as his Max's gumshield exploded out of his mouth with and eruption of blood and saliva and then skittered across the floor of the ring.

Max's guard was completely down, and his arms hung at his side as he tottered backwards. Miles stepped forward to deliver a right uppercut, which connected with Max's chin and lifted him off his feet.

"Fucking hell Miles!" shouted Mick as he propped Max in the corner wiping his bloody nose with a wet towel and holding smelling salts under his nostrils. "You were supposed to be sparring, you've half killed him."

Miles stared for a moment at Max's prone form and then turned and stepped through the ropes of the ring pulling at the Velcro fastenings of his gloves. He laid them on the shelf, picked up his hoody and kitbag and headed for the door without looking back.

Two weeks later at the next Millwall game Miles went with Charlie and stood where he always had. He saw the guy handing out kidney donor cards to the away fans and smirking. Miles didn't smile.

Since leaving school Miles had been stocking shelves in Sainsburys on Peckham High Street. He was looking for something better and his dad promised to ask around Smithfield to see if there were any openings for him, but it was his mum who came up with the goods.

One evening whilst beginning her cleaning duties at the offices of Surety and Guarantee, Sharon Dixon had come across the Head of Underwriting, Barry Teyford, sitting at his desk working late.

Barry was a South London boy too and had a soft spot for Sharon, as indeed he did for the rest of the women in the office. Sharon had told Barry about Miles and he said that there was a vacancy in the Post Room. "You won't have to get up in the middle of the night," she said when she came home. "They don't start until 9.30 and you get Luncheon vouchers."

Miles had started the next week. Through delivering the post everyday he got to know almost all the 200 or so employees at the head office of Surety and Guarantee. They were a very mixed bunch. Most of the Directors were from Public School and the Forces, the majority of which lived in the Home Counties. Miles noticed that the Marketing Director was never there on a Tuesday or Thursday. "Is he just part-time?" he asked the Director's secretary. "Oh no, he's full time, but he's the Master of the Quorn Hunt and they ride on Tuesday and Thursday," she smiled as if that explained everything.

The people who dealt with clients, the underwriters and the account managers, were much more like Miles. Most came from the East End, at least originally, and had moved further out into Essex as they became more successful in their career. Most were below the age of 40 and had similar interests to Miles.

Soon Miles found that he had a new set of friends and it helped that Barry Teyford took him under his wing and explained over a lengthy series of conversations in his office how the world of credit insurance worked.

At first Miles had almost no idea about business. He had no experience of the world of commerce. His dad chopped up cows and his mum mopped floors. They certainly hadn't taught him anything at school where his experience of manufacture and production pretty much stopped at dovetail joints. He didn't even know what an invoice was.

At first Profit and Loss Statements and Balance Sheets, which made up Company Accounts, were incomprehensible. Barry Teyford almost invariably had his head buried in their pages when Miles stopped to deliver the post each day. To him they looked like a tangled mass of figures. But with his grasp of maths and Barry patiently taking the time to explain the intricacies of the numbers Miles came to understand how to assess a company's worth based on this information.

"This is what Surety and Guarantee do," Barry said to Miles. "Economies revolve around the use of trade credit. If say, you are a watch manufacturer your route to market will most likely to be jewellery shops. Now these shops won't want to pay you for your goods until they have had a chance to sell them and make some money for themselves. So usually you have to offer credit terms which means you won't get paid for at least 30 days from delivering the watches." Barry pulled on a cigarette as he watched Miles nod in understanding.

"In turn you will ask the people who supply you with the components to make the watches for credit too because you are waiting for payment from the jewellery shops. It's a chain of trust and expectation and this all works out well if people do what they have promised." Barry exhaled smoke from his nose.

"But what happens if one of the jewellery shops you are supplying goes bust?" He raised his eyebrows in question. "Well, if you have only supplied them with a few watches you may be able to absorb the debt. On the other hand, if they are a big customer, then the money that you need to pay your suppliers isn't forthcoming and you too may have to declare bankruptcy.

"Credit insurance covers this possibility, but it isn't without certain checks and balances. The main thing we do is investigate the background of the companies you are supplying to make sure that they have the money to pay for the goods. The Report and Accounts of a company will tell us that and if they are a limited company they have to file accounts every year and it's every six months for a PLC."

"So how come Surety and Guarantee pay out any claims if they have already checked out the financial worth of a company?" Miles asked.

Barry smiled. He had expected this question. "First of all, young Miles, the accounts can be old. Let's say your financial year ends on 31st December. A company must have time to prepare these accounts and Companies House allows ten months from the end of the financial year to file them. That means that they don't become available for public inspection until 1st October the following year. A company then has another year before it has to file a fresh set of accounts so, quite legally, the information can be up to 22 months old."

Barry smiled at the surprise on the young man's face.

"Now, the financial worth of a company might have changed fundamentally in that time. Maybe they have had a bad debt, or their largest customer has stopped ordering from them. Maybe the owner has been seriously ill, or their factory has burned down. Any number of factors can have changed in that time, but the information you are reading in the accounts still says they can pay their bills on time but maybe in reality they can't. It's like looking at a star that burned out millions of years ago but you can still see its reflection in the sky."

Miles nodded his head and looked thoughtful.

"Also, the Report and Accounts of a company are as much a matter of interpretation than anything else. Yes, we can see the sales and the costs of the business, provided the numbers are truthful, but what about everything else? What happens if you own a factory which in the Balance Sheet is valued at a million pounds but, in fact, is only worth half a million? Then you have just added £500k to the value of that company entirely spuriously! But it's not illegal: it's a matter of opinion.

"Clever accountants charge businesses thousands of pounds a day to make one thing look like another. Our job is to try and read between the lines and see if any evasion is practiced but it's an art not a science and is learned mainly through experience."

"But if a company goes bust the Directors are struck off and aren't allowed to trade again, right?" said Miles.

Barry laughed. "Oh poor, sweet, innocent boy. The word "Limited" in a company title means the Directors only risk what they have invested in a company. If they go bust the Directors aren't responsible for the debts they leave behind, they don't have to sell their house or anything. They can hand over the running of the company to an insolvency practitioner who can sell the company on or liquidate its assets. And if a company is sold on to new owners who do you think they are?" asked Barry smiling mischievously.

"As often as not, the Directors of the company that just went bust," Barry laughed.

"Quite often they arrange with the Insolvency Practitioner to buy the company back the very next day. It's called a pre-packaged administration or "prepack" for short. The previous owners have just bought their own company back but don't have to pay any of the suppliers who are out of pocket. They are free to trade without the liabilities of the old company to hold them back.

"The only time Directors get struck off is if they are found to have behaved illegally and the times that happens in a year, I can count on the fingers of one hand. The Fraud Squad just don't have the time or resources to deal with the vast majority of this stuff. They tend to go after high profile cases. If you want to do this there's a 99.9% chance you will get away with it. Just ask Reggie and Ronnie Kray."

"That can't be right," Miles said, shaking his head.

"That's Capitalism mate," said Barry and winked at him.

With Barry's support and his wide range of contacts within Surety and Guarantee it was not long before Miles got his foot on the underwriting ladder.

One of the clerical staff had resigned just before Christmas. The beginning of January was often the busiest time of year for the company with many of their clients beginning their new financial year at the start of the month. There was no time to advertise, interview and train a replacement from outside the business so Miles got the job without having to go through any of the formalities.

In the years that followed Miles worked in every department in Surety and Guarantee. It was like being on the graduate training scheme but knowing how to work the photocopier too he used to joke.

Miles had met Kath at work. They had married and moved out to Romford and Kath had given up work when Evie was born which was just after Miles had been promoted to be head of claims at the age of 35.

 In the nineteen years that had elapsed Miles thought he had seen it all and done it all. He had developed a nose for the business as Barry used to describe it, he could spot what was genuine and what was an attempt to deceive which the Board of Directors thought was an important quality in the man who signed the claim's cheques.

Chapter 5

Two days after his release Jaimie was sitting in a pub in Ashton Lane. It was a Saturday afternoon and the Scotland versus England rugby match was on the television. Rugby was not Jaimie's game. He was a football man but there was no live soccer on the TV and he had nothing better to do.

He had been settled in a corner since opening time. It was raining outside, and he had nowhere to go. He listened to the crowd at Murrayfield sing the national anthem. He loved "Flower of Scotland," it's rhythm like a heartbeat. "Oh, flower of Scotland, boom, boom, When will we see thee rise again?" It was a lot better than the bloody Sassenach anthem that doesn't even mention England. In fact, the only country mentioned in "God Save the Queen," is Scotland or at least it's rebellious inhabitants.

Jaimie took the last sip from his pint of heavy. He had been in the pub for three hours already and yet he had only just finished his second glass. He was not used to drinking. Occasionally, people would smuggle half bottles of vodka into the Centre, but dope and pills had been easier, and he had mainly existed on those when he had wanted to get out of it.

He needed a piss. He got up and headed to the toilets. When he came back, two men were sitting at the table he had occupied.

"Sorry pal, you dinnae realise that I was sitting here," said Jaimie, tapping the table with his fist.

The two men looked at him. They were about the same age as Jaimie and both wore rugby shirts.

"I don't think so pal, there was naybody here when we sat doon," said the man on the left.

"Aye, I see that," said Jaimie, "but I had to piss. I've been gone two minutes no more."

"And how are we supposed to know that? The table was empty. Nae glasses, nae coat over the chair. Nothing." The man sitting in Jaimie's vacated seat was beginning to bristle and the other guy looked like he was ready to fight too.

"Aye, I suppose you're right," said Jaimie and began to turn away.

"Now fuck off," said the man on the left as he lifted his pint to his mouth. Jaimie heard the other man snigger. He turned and pushed the pint glass into the man's face and headbutted his friend as he rose from his seat.

It took four guys to restrain Jaimie while they waited for the police. The two men he had injured were regulars and he had taken quite a kicking before two constables arrived.

During the following police interview he found out that one of the men may have lost the sight in his left eye. Jaimie was put on remand. When his case came up, he was found guilty of GBH and sentenced to two years. In theory, he was still too young for adult prison but given his record of violence it was deemed necessary to send him to Barlinnie where he could be held in solitary confinement if required and where he was likely to learn a harsh lesson from the screws and the other inmates.

Jaimie was taken straight from the High Court to prison. He was processed. This involved being strip-searched and then made to squat to ensure no drugs had been stuffed in his rectum. He was then put in a holding room where he was weighed and measured, and a medical history was taken.

It was six hours before a warder led him to a cell. Under his arm was a "welcome pack" with a sheet, a pillow, an orange blanket, a toothbrush and toothpaste, a plastic cup, a fork, knife and spoon and some prison soap. He could hear the wolf whistles and the catcalls as he walked down the block. He was thin and pale. He barely looked nineteen. He was the youngest man in Barlinnie and would be a target for the nonces.

In the cell he was shown into an older man was lying on the top bunk. Jaimie guessed he was around forty. As the door was locked by the warder Jaimie arranged his possessions on the spare lower bunk. Amongst the Welcome Pack he had been given a bag of sweets. He threw them away angrily. He heard a rustle from the top bunk and looked up. He saw a hand hanging down. "Simon Lebowitz, pleased to meet you," came a voice. It was heavily accented. Foreign. Not English foreign, but properly foreign. Jaimie ignored the proffered hand and it was withdrawn.

The walk to his cell on the first day had just been the opening moves in a game of intimidation.

The prisoners were locked up for 23 hours a day, but they were allowed out for meals. The hour where the men were not confined was spent in the recreation yard. Jaimie was aware that he was being stared out for every minute that he was outside his cell. A group of five men would make clucking noises at him whenever he was in hearing distance and if he stared back at them, he was greeted by fluttering eyelashes and kisses being blown. Despite them being nonces, they looked large and powerful. They were not the effeminate and fey men Jaimie expected.

On the second day at 6.30 Jaimie was let out of his cell and made his way to the Mess Hall for breakfast. He carried his cup and set of plastic utensils. He stood in line and collected his food on a tray with compartments. Porridge, toast and tea.

He had spoken to nobody since he arrived. He looked for a spare table to eat his food. At the first one he stopped at he was told to "fuck off." He eventually found a table, which was empty and sat down. He ate his food not looking up. He was aware of other men sitting down around him, but he ignored them.

"Hello, sweetie," came a man's voice from opposite him. Still, he kept on eating his head down. "We have all been looking forward to meeting you," the voice continued. He heard murmurs of agreement. "You look brand new. Lovely and tight, although you won't be by the time, we've finished with you." He heard laughter and felt the foot of the man opposite rubbing along the inside of his calf. Jaimie now looked up and gave the man a cold stare. "Fuck off," he said.

The man was fat, perhaps 250 pounds, with hooded eyes. He looked swarthy. Jaimie could smell his body odour. "Don't be like that darling, or we'll knock all of your teeth out." The man smiled back at him, but Jaimie could see the menace in his eyes. "You won't look so pretty but it'd be better for blow jobs."

Jaimie had picked up his fork. He thrust it at the man's eye. It was only plastic but would still have made a hell of a mess if it had connected with the eye socket he was aiming for. The man turned his head and the plastic prongs bent as they met his cheek. He screamed. Jaimie jumped to his feet and punched the man twice in the side of his head. He looked up to see the screws running towards him their batons drawn. He stepped back and put his hands up in the air. That was a fight that he could not win.

He had been taken straight to the Governor's office and awarded a week in solitary confinement. "You shouldn't have done that to Righty. He's vicious and so are his friends," smiled the screw as he led him into the cell.

There was just a mattress on the floor and a bare lightbulb. The window was up high in the wall, so he would not be able to look out of it. The screw was enjoying Jaimie's discomfort. "It's always best to let the nonces have their way, they soon get fed up and move on to someone else. There is always fresh meat in Barlinnie," he laughed and then winked.

Jaimie could not believe what he was hearing. It seemed that the authorities were happy to turn a blind eye to what in his eyes was the worst crime you could commit. It should be those bastards in solitary confinement, not him. Permanently. Were the screws members of the same secret club too?

The seven days passed by slowly. Jaimie's emotions seesawed between fear and violent fantasies of revenge. He was not scared of violence, but rape was another matter. He wondered if he would be able to fend off five guys particularly if the screws were willing to be somewhere else when an attack happened?

He would rather be dead than to allow these men to inflict their perversions on him, he decided. As the screw said, once they had had their fun, they would probably leave him alone. Sex like this was a way of asserting authority. If these men just wanted sex, they could just fuck each other. This was about dominance. It was about power: once it was established, they would look to grow their twisted empire elsewhere.

What they would leave behind though was the empty husk of a man. No, he would fight with his last breath to stop that. He wished he had Jimmy's combat knife.

A week later Jaimie was led back to his cell. He heard the catcalls and whistles behind him and the muttered threats. When he entered, Simon Lebowitz was sitting on the top bunk. He was listening to some classical shit on his transistor radio and reading a large book. Before he had been put in solitary Jaimie had to endure hours of classical music and programmes with people talking in posh English voices about stuff that he did not understand. Why couldn't his cellmate listen to Radio 1 like everybody else?

Lebowitz looked up. "So, you're back?" he smiled. Jaimie ignored him. He was probably a nonce too but was trying to get what he wanted by pretending to be kind rather than just taking it.

"What you did was brave, but you need to be careful. Don't go anywhere where they can get you by yourself. It might be a good idea if you shit your pants. It puts them off and then you are just likely to get a beating. Stay down wind of me if you do though." Lebowitz returned to reading his book.

For the next ten days Jaimie spent almost every hour in the cell. They were locked up for 23 hours a day anyway, but he avoided going to the recreation yard. When he went to get his meals, he ate them quickly, standing up and walking towards the mess entrance as he shovelled the food into his mouth.

Twice a week the prisoners were given an opportunity for a shower, but he remained in his cell. He would use the slop bucket rather than go to the toilets. He was beginning to smell. Lebowitz would bring him back a cup of water after each meal and he tried to wash in that, using the edge of his towel as a flannel. As he stood dabbing at his armpits one morning his cellmate looked over the top of his newspaper at him. "Sooner or later you are going to have to face up to this, young man," he said. "You can't run away forever."

Later that day Jaimie went to the mess hall. He found a table and sat down. Nobody came to sit with him. In his peripheral vision he could see other inmates looking at him as he ate. He finished and walked back to his cell. There were no catcalls or obscene threats shouted at him. Perhaps the nonces had found another victim?

The following Tuesday, Jaimie made his way to the shower block. He followed Lebowitz into the changing room, stripped off and hung his clothes on a hook. The room was full of steam. It smelt of Deep Heat and cigarettes. He looked around nervously. There were no nonces to be seen. Maybe they had finished already?

He walked into the communal shower. There were three others in there. His cellmate was washing his hair. He felt refreshed as the hot water sprayed over him. He ripped open the sachet of shampoo he had been given and lathered it into his hair. He closed his eyes to stop the suds stinging them. He washed his arse, his crotch and his groin, something that he had been desperate to do.

When he opened his eyes Lebowitz had gone and so had everybody else. Standing at the entrance to the shower were three of the nonces, fully clothed. He looked behind him and blocking the other exit were the other two.

One of them came towards him and Jaimie swung a headbutt towards his face. It connected with the man's nose and blood spurted from both nostrils. He could feel two hands grip his lower arms from behind. He reversed the headbutt and could feel his skull contact something hard: it felt like the man's chin.

After that his memories became confused. He remembered slipping on the soapy wet floor, his fists flailing and biting somebody. Then he fell. His head cracked against the glazed wall. He was lying on the wet tiles, his head spinning. Righty was standing over him grinning evilly. Then he saw a booted foot smash into the side of the man's head.

Through the steam he could see the blurry vision of Simon Lebowitz lifting his bent arm and smashing down onto another man's collarbone. He heard a crack and a scream. Then he passed out.

Lebowitz smiled at him when he was taken back to his cell. He had regained consciousness in the Medical Bay and after a couple of hours of observation a screw had taken him back to C Wing. He was confused. He was certain that he would be dragged back in front of the Governor and then thrown into solitary confinement again.

"That was very impressive," said Lebowitz. "You have potential."

"I saw you kick Righty," he said. "Thanks."

Lebowitz laughed. "You did most of the work yourself. One has a broken nose, another has smashed teeth and biting that guy's cock was inspired."

Jaimie shook his head weakly. "I don't understand," he said.

"One of the bastards had his tool out. Already to give it to you and you bit a bloody great chunk out of the end." He was wheezing with laughter now. "He's lost so much of his foreskin his cock probably looks like mine." Jaimie didn't get it. Was Lebowitz coming on to him?

"Anyway, three of them are still in the hospital and the other two are in solitary nursing their injuries. I'm surprised you didn't see them?" his cellmate said.

Jaimie explained that he had been kept in the Medical Room under observation. "I don't understand why I am not in trouble though?" he said.

"As soon as the fight was over all the nonces took off. Well, limped away," Lebowitz smiled. "The screws turn a blind eye to sex attacks, but the Governor takes it seriously. The two in solitary must be there because it has been assumed they had been fighting each other. I washed the blood away and then called the screws. I said that you had slipped in the shower."

Chapter 6

Miles first met Kath when she pogoed on his foot.

It was 1977, and punk had exploded. Until then, Miles had always been a soul boy. Dressed in high-waisted baggies, pod toed shoes, shirts with huge collars and hideous jumpers he had always considered himself to be at the forefront of sophisticated youth.

As he stood in the Marquee Club in Oxford Street watching the Clash belt out "White Riot": one minute and fifty-eight seconds of pure joy, he realized that he had been wrong. He still loved the Motown, Stax and Atlantic records of the 1960s but this music spoke to him in a different way. It reflected things he experienced every day: living in a flat, being poor, getting your head kicked in for looking at somebody in the wrong way.

The promise of the Swinging '60s had dissipated. Britain in the 1970s was dirty and broken. Civil strife existed everywhere from Northern Ireland to the picket lines manned by miners, car worker and postmen. Governments with slim majorities frequently came and went exhausted by the seemingly insoluble problems of hyper-inflation, industrial unrest and growing unemployment. The three-day week was a reflection of a country whose inhabitants were at each other's throats.

As Slade sang "Merry Christmas Everybody" for the first time, the Prime Minister, Edward Heath was busy switching off the country's lights, heating and television. The foreign press called the UK "the sick man of Europe."

The lack of leadership was accompanied by a lack of money and in a state of near bankruptcy the country borrowed from the International Monetary Fund in 1976. British manufactured goods were a by-word for shoddy and yet nobody cared because nobody cared about them. Society was blinkered and insular.

Meals were an endless round of meat, gravy and potatoes. Pasta, olive oil and garlic were "foreign food," a description always accompanied with a disgusted shudder. A celebratory dinner at a Berni Inn was inevitably a glass of orange juice as a starter and a burned steak for the main. Those seeking more variety in their diet were warned that the Indian and Chinese restaurants cooked rats and domestic animals.

In the towns there was nothing to do. On Friday and Saturday nights young people met in dirty pubs to drink horrible beer and then be sent home at half past ten by a pinched faced landlord who begrudged them his hospitality even though they had spent all their money on his warm pints of piss. On Sundays the country was closed: every High Street grey, windswept and abandoned because the churches said that Sunday was special; and it was special, but not in a good way.

The people in the crowd that night were young and angry. They were the representatives of a system that discriminated against the working class, women and immigrants. If you were born in the wrong circumstances then your life was mapped out for you: the factory, the building sites or the mines. Now and then they would allow people to escape, to better themselves: to prove that it could be done; but not many.

Disaffection and violence was everywhere. It was manifested in the youth tribes of skinheads, boot boys and greasers, in football violence and in the graffiti on the soot stained walls of London. Punk captured this frustration. Although mainly sung by white men, it incorporated black music too. Not the happy-clappy Motown stuff but something from somewhere much darker. The sound of oppression. The sound of Jamaica, Notting Hill and Brixton. Reggae, dub and ska.

Joe Strummer had slowed it down now for "Police and Thieves," half the words incomprehensible sung through his amphetamine-wrecked teeth. The chaka-chaka of Mick Jones's guitar, the rumble of Paul Simonon's bass.

Miles looked around. Nobody had long hair. Nobody had the spiked Mohicans beloved by the second generation of punks either: the idiots of the early eighties that Miles later came to hate. Posers who stood on the Kings Road drinking Special Brew and charging tourists for photographs.

No, these were the early days. Most lads were dressed in their dad's gardening jackets with a few safety pins, maybe some kids' pink sunglasses for effect; their flared Levi's taken in on their mum's sewing machines to become drainpipes. Some of the girls wore binbags and ripped tights, pink, green and peroxide hair.

Miles had first heard of punk rock when watching the local news magazine programme for London, called Today. It was in December of the previous year. The presenter was an insipid middle age man named Bill Grundy. He was the type of colourless character who normally presented the local news.

That night, for some strange reason, he was interviewing a pop group called the Sex Pistols. Miles had never heard of them. The band had four members. They did not look like normal bands. They were young, but they all had short hair. All of Miles's mates, in fact everybody at school, including the teachers, had long hair.

One of the band, who seemed to be the spokesman, was smoking and was wearing a tee-shirt with a pair of women's tits emblazoned on the front. Another, with dyed red hair, looked like a rat. The girls standing behind the band all had short, cropped hair. One looked like a Pierrot doll, another was wearing a swastika armband.

What was most amazing was the way they swore. Nobody ever swore on teatime television. In fact, nobody ever really swore on television at all. There was the odd "bloody" and a very occasional "bastard," but you normally had to wait until after nine o'clock to hear language like that. In two minutes, these boys had managed to rack up two "shits, one "sod," one "bastard," and three different ways of using the word "fuck."

Miles was amazed. You didn't get this from The Bay City Rollers, he thought. His dad was laughing, but his mum kept shaking her head and saying "disgraceful." She looked at Miles and Charlie, who were sniggering. "I hope you don't talk like that?" Both boys shook their heads in mock innocence. Sharon gave Harry a withering look, which made him laugh louder.

The next day, Miles bought a copy of the Daily Mirror. He had noticed the headline "TV Fury Over Rock Cult Filth." He excitedly read the transcript of the previous night's interview. It said that one man had put his foot through his TV set because he was so annoyed.

That weekend, Miles went to Woolworth's in Peckham High Street and bought a copy of the Sex Pistol's single, "Anarchy in the UK." He waited until his parents were out until putting on the Radiogram in the flat. He was stunned at what he heard. Fast and pounding with a sneering lyric it referenced things he heard about on the news every might: the IRA, the UDA, the MPLA. From then on, all other pop music became vapid, over produced nonsense written by fat, middle-aged men who had no idea what it was like to be 15. Well, he still liked David Bowie, but that was about all.

Punk was not played on the radio. The smarmy DJs with their stupid phone-in quizzes and daily recipes seemed to despise it. Miles had to wait until late at night. Lying under the bed cover with a transistor pressed to his ear he would listen to the John Peel show. Only he would play this new wave of music: the do-it-yourself tapes sent in from bands formed in the surge of euphoria and stuff from pub bands that had rejected stadium rock, Dr. Feelgood and Eddie and the Hot Rods.

In his English lesson, Mr. Bowen, had read out a poem by William Wordsworth. It had the line:

"Bliss it was in that dawn to be alive. But to be young was very heaven."

Mr. Bowen said it was about the French Revolution that had happened two hundred years before, but for Miles it equally applied to the English revolution that was happening then.

The whole movement had come from the street. The touch paper was the Sex Pistols, but instantaneously disaffected youths understood it and flocked to its banner. It was the music of alienation but also of belonging. Paul Weller's line: "Tears of rage run down your face, but still you say it's fun," was true.

There were not many punk records by that stage. The only way really to listen was to go and see the bands play live at venues mainly in the West End. That was easy for Miles. He could cycle there, his punk gear hidden in a plastic shopping bag because he knew that his parents would not approve. He would get changed in the toilet of any pub near that night's venue. The gigs were mainly at the weekend, so his mum did not mind if he was out until midnight.

That night, he found himself at the Marquee Club. The Clash ripped into "Garageland." Beer sprayed around as kids pogoed and spat.

A girl in front of him was jumping up and down. She was dressed in a leather motorcycle jacket with tight black jeans. Her eyes were heavily made up with black eyeliner, which came into points making her seem oriental. She was black, with short cropped hair and green eyes, which flashed in the strobe lights. Miles thought she looked like Cat Woman from Batman. She landed heavily on his toe. Miles was annoyed. He was wearing a brand-new pair of brothel creepers: his blue suede shoes.

"Oi, fuckin' mind out!" he shouted down her ear.

The girl looked at him, smiled, flicked a V-sign and pogoed off into the crowd.

He saw Cat Woman a lot that summer. At the Roxy watching Chelsea and Slaughter and the Dogs. At the Hope and Anchor watching X-Ray Spex. She always smiled and flicked the V-sign at him. Miles used to laugh. She was pretty. He tried to talk to her a few times, but she was there to watch the band and dance, not to pick up boys.

Harry, Miles's dad, liked his son's new look although he could not abide the music. "It's about time you got your hair cut. You were beginning to look like a poodle," he said.

Harry's style was 1950s Rat Pack. He looked a bit like Dean Martin in those days. On Saturday nights he would be off out in a sharkskin suit, white button-down shirt and thin black tie. His mum, Sharon, used to look like Debbie Reynolds. They were a handsome couple. His dad would finish every night at the boozer singing "My Way," or "Mack the Knife."

Sharon liked Miles's new look too. "He looks like Eddie Cochran," she would say. Although, when he brought home "God Save the Queen," by the Sex Pistols she refused to make him his dinner at night until he managed to swap it for a copy of "Where Have All the Boot Boys Gone?" at school. Charlie, his brother, continued to lock himself in his bedroom and listen to Emerson, Lake and Palmer.

On his first day working for Surety and Guarantee, Miles was delivering some mail to the Marketing Department. He smiled at the girl who was the assistant in that department. She looked vaguely familiar, but he could not decide where he had seen her before. "Well, if it isn't Sid Vicious," she said. It was Cat Woman. She introduced herself as Kath. "At least you didn't flick the V-sign at me," said Miles. "I only do it behind people's backs at work," she smiled.

Kath Hendricks had been born in Brixton. Her dad, Selwyn, had sailed over in 1948 on the S.S. Empire Windrush.

At first, he had lived in Notting Hill in the slums owned by Peter Rachman. He occupied a single room in an old Georgian house separated out into bedsitters with a sink, cooker and a toilet on each landing to be shared by all the residents of that floor. He saw people being turned out of their rooms with a minute's notice.

Rachman would hold snarling Alsatians on a lead who growled and bit the retreating evictees as they hauled their possessions down the stairs to the street where inevitably they would meet a new family waiting to occupy their abandoned room for a higher rent.

In the windows of other boarding houses, he saw the signs "No Blacks, No Dogs, No Irish." In certain shops they refused to serve him.

Selwyn had left Jamaica to join the RAF during the war. He was a mechanic, servicing Lancaster bombers. In those days he drank with the white personnel in the mess. There was the odd joke about golliwogs that he had to endure but mostly it was in a friendly spirit. In those days the British were desperate for people to help them win the war. When he returned to England it seemed they had forgotten the contribution of the West Indies. People would spit the words "wog," "nignog," "coon" and "black bastard" at him.

Selwyn was a qualified engineer but the only jobs he could get were menial ones. He ended up working as a bus driver.

Despite the hostility of most of the white population there were a few that would treat him as an equal. Every day he bought his lunch from a café opposite the depot. There was a young woman who worked behind the counter there. She was called Mary. She was from Ireland and lily white, as Selwyn later used to laugh. Her intentions towards the strong, Jamaican man were made plain and they married in 1956.

Three years later, they moved to Brixton after a group of three hundred young, white men, mainly Teddy Boys, moved through their neighbourhood in Notting Hill assaulting any West Indian men they found and smashing up any property inhabited by blacks.

Selwyn had read about the 1938 Kristallnacht, or the Night of Broken Glass, in Germany when Hitler's thugs did the same to Jewish homes, shops and synagogues. He could not help but draw comparisons. It seemed that the British had fought the Germans but not the Nazis. He decided to move to Brixton where most people were West Indian; where his wife would not receive the vile abuse that she did in the streets and the shops of west London for being seen with a black man.

Kath was Selwyn's eldest daughter. She came to punk through her brother, Delroy's, love of reggae.

Delroy was a year older than her. Throughout her formative years Kath remembered the sounds of Dillinger and Prince Buster creeping under her brother's bedroom door. On Saturdays she would accompany him to the record stall in the Railton Road to sort through boxes of records imported from Jamaica.

In 1973 Delroy had caught the first appearance of Bob Marley and the Wailers late one Tuesday night on the Old Grey Whistle Test. It was to radically alter his appearance and attitude. Overnight his style changed from the Superfly of Shaft to a Rastafarian convert. His south London accent had been replaced by the thick patois of Kingston, Jamaica.

Delroy grew his hair into dreadlocks often wrapped up into a red, gold and green woollen hat. He believed that Rastas were the lost tribe of Israel and that their destiny was to return to Ethiopia to worship Emperor Haile Selassie, who was the manifestation of Jesus Christ returned to Earth. The fact that Haile Selassie, the so-called Lion of Judea, had been deposed in a coup did not seem to matter.

Kath thought that Rastafarianism was just an excuse to smoke dope. She did not like their belief that women on their periods were considered unclean and were to be avoided. Her Rasta boyfriends were quick enough to shove their hands up her skirt at any other time though. She spent hours arguing about this with her brother and his friends but felt that her point was always ignored. They called her "sister," but they treated her more like a chattel.

So many of her friends had literally been left holding the baby by men like her brother who seemed to believe it was their duty to scatter their seed widely but never to sow it. By the age of sixteen, Delroy already had two kids by two different women. Like Moses with his ten commandments, Marcus Garvey had told the Rastas how things were, and they had accepted it unquestioningly. Kath knew she would never adopt this new religion. Delroy was determined to change his sister's mind.

In July,1975 he took her to the Lyceum in Covent Garden to see Bob Marley and the Wailers play live for the first time in England. For Kath the music was not like the stuff she watched on Top of the Pops. It was not just the rhythm but the subject of the songs that was different. There was no "I love you, do you love me?" theme. Marley with his eyes closed, dreads swinging sang songs with titles like "Burnin' and Lootin, 'Concrete Jungle," and "Them Belly Full (But We Hungry)" as he marched, high stepping on the spot.

Kath could empathise with the sentiments of the words. The boys in her neighbourhood were constantly stopped and searched by the police who felt entitled to abuse them in the most derogatory and humiliating ways. Later, this was a spark to the Notting Hill riots in

1976. The following year, she witnessed the National Front march through Lewisham: a procession of smirking skinheads led by a fat, effeminate man in a raincoat.

As Kath looked around, she noticed that although most of the audience were black there were little knots of white people in the audience, mainly boys. Delroy would hiss "raasclaat" at them if any came too close. Raasclaat was the favourite Jamaican insult, meaning sanitary towel. Why were these boys so obsessed with women's periods?

"You silly bastard, mum's white!" said Kath shoving her brother. Delroy sucked his teeth audibly. It seemed to him that you had to be on one side or the other. Kath did not buy that. It was all too easy to cast yourself in the role of victim.

She had read about Martin Luther King in school. The plight of American blacks had been terrible and yet, unlike others, he had chosen the path of non-violence and integration and not separation and bloodshed.

King had been inspired by Gandhi, and Kath held dear his maxim that if you wanted to change the world then first change yourself. Even Malcolm X who had called white men "blue-eyed devils" had come to see a better way before he died. So, although most Rastas objected to sharing their beloved prophet, Bob Marley, with duppies, Kath saw a mixed audience as a positive thing. It was not only black people who felt the need for change.

Kath Hendricks had always been creative. By the mid-1970s she was enrolled as student at Saint Martin's School of Art. Like the birth of British rock 'n' roll in the '50s and '60s, Punk Rock had been fomented in the

Common Rooms of Art Schools. It addressed the same subjects as reggae but, to Kath, was embracing of all. One love. Only the punks did not care if she was a girl. Only the punks did not care if she was mixed race, or half-caste as most whites called it then, as if, somehow, she had been spoiled in the manufacturing process.

By the end of the '70s she had completed her degree in design and secured a job at Surety and Guarantee.

Miles Dixon would look forward to delivering the mail to her everyday and they would talk about music and films. Their first date was to see "Sid and Nancy" at the Odeon in Leicester Square. Miles moved in with Kath a few months later to her little rented flat in Newington Green. They married two years after that. Their first dance was to the Billy Idol's "White Wedding."

For the first few years, life as a white boy and a black girl was not easy. Miles had always been aware of the National Front hanging around Millwall's ground on matchdays handing out leaflets comparing black people to apes.

The boys in F Troop had been exclusively white and they were happy to chant abuse at any black players who played for the visiting team. Kath loved football but often taking her to watch Millwall was an ordeal, from the hostile stares in the street to the monkey noises coming from behind you in the crowd which would stop as soon as he turned around.

Harry and Sharon adored Kath though. Neither of them ever mentioned her colour. In fact, Miles could never remember either of them uttering a racist sentiment. Miles and his brother were named after two black men: Miles Davis and Charlie Parker, his dad's jazz heroes. Harry had no truck with racism at all.

His father had travelled to Spain in 1936 to fight for the Republican cause. He had brought Harry up to reject fascism in all its forms. Anybody who indulged in cheap epithets around him got very short shrift. In the market, the pub and at Coldblow Lane people would know when to shut up if he was nearby. The first time Miles ever heard the word "wankers" was when Harry was watching the television news one night and there was a report about the London dockworkers going on strike in support of Enoch Powell.

Over the years though things gradually improved. Miles would take Kath to see Millwall at the New Den. People no longer seemed to notice or care that a white man was sitting with a black girl. After the match they would go to the pub with Harry and then roll back to his old home in Peckham Rye for tea on a Saturday night.

Every time they visited though, Miles's mum and dad kept asking when they were going to start a family. They always used to laugh it off and said that they were too busy working. The truth was that they had been trying for ages. Miles had been promoted a few times and they could afford for Kath to give up work. They had even moved at to Essex in expectation of Kath getting pregnant.

They went for tests at the hospital. It seemed that nothing was medically wrong with either of them. It became an obsession. Kath would take a pregnancy test every month. It would be negative every time. She would cry and become depressed for days. Miles felt guilty. If anything could complete their life it would be a baby.

After two years of trying to conceive, they gave up. Sensing their embarrassment, his parents stopped mentioning grandchildren. It existed like a chasm between the young couple. Unspoken, but always there: a heart-breaking yearning. For years they simply lived with the emptiness.

One summer's day they met Kath's sister, Jess, and her husband, John, for a picnic in Hyde Park. Jess and John had a little girl, Roxie, their niece. It was Roxie's third birthday. Her exhausted parents sat on the picnic rug drinking wine as Miles and Kath chased the giggling toddler around the park. They took her to the swings and on the slide. They bought her ice cream.

Miles noticed how Kath could not stop touching the little girl. She hugged her, kissed her and held her hand. All the time she was laughing and smiling, but in the car home she was sad, listless and withdrawn. Miles was too.

He decided that they should investigate fertility treatment. Kath was 37 now. Time was running out. It might be expensive, but he could no longer see his wife this unhappy. They ordered all the brochures and arranged an appointment with a specialist at a private clinic. Then one day just before the appointment, things changed.

Kath had not gone to work that day. In the morning she had said that she did not feel well. When Miles arrived home his wife was in tears. He could see from her face that she had been crying for hours. He dropped his briefcase and knelt beside her as she sat on the sofa. "I'm pregnant," she said. The pair sat holding each other intermittently sobbing with relief and smiling with joy.

Evie was born at Guy's Hospital early one morning in January. The birth was quick and uncomplicated. She was perfect with a big patch of dark hair like her mother. Miles and Kath felt their life was complete.

They wanted nothing else than this beautiful little girl. When Harry and Sharon visited, they both cried. Miles had never seen his dad cry before; a big man reduced to an emotional wreck by the baby that lay in his arms. He vowed then that Evie would always be happy and always be safe.

Chapter 7

Simon Lebowitz was 43 years old. He had been born on a kibbutz in Israel in the year that country had been founded. His mother was English. His father, Samuel, was Polish, the last remaining survivor of an extended family which in 1940 had numbered over one hundred members. They had come from Lwow.

Before the outbreak of World War Two the city was home to over 110,000 Jews. By the time the Nazis occupied the city in 1941 that number had doubled with Jews fleeing for their lives from German-occupied western Poland. With the occupation of Lwow came the Einsatzgruppen, the death squads of the Third Reich.

They murdered those Jews who were "uneconomic" to keep. Samuel remembered peering from a high window in the factory he worked at. He saw the old and infirm standing in single lines in front of a pit they had been forced to dig and heard the endless crack of rifle fire all day as the victims lurched forward into the muddy hole. They were replaced by a fresh batch, herded into place with rifle butts and snarling dogs.

Samuel had worked as a slave making casements for artillery shells. Within a few months the Nazis had established a ghetto where all Jews were required to live. It was cut off from the rest of Lwow by barbed wire fences and armed guards.

One day in 1942, he and the rest of his workmates were taken from the factory and loaded on a train to Janowska Concentration Camp. They were forced to work at the Eastern Railway Repair Works painting swastikas and other inscriptions on captured Soviet railway engines. The barracks for the workers were outside the main facility.

In September 1943, Samuel was able to escape. A work party had been taken outside the camp to repair some railway tracks. It was raining heavily that day and as the procession of workers turned a corner on the track back to the camp he simply disappeared into the forest; because of the weather the guards did not notice until the journey had been completed.

After hiding out for a few days Samuel was able to contact the Polish underground. They hid him at various houses until he was discovered by the Gestapo eight months later. He was hiding in a closet in the home of a partisan. He was taken back to Janowska to find that most of the camp's inhabitants had been "liquidated," the Nazi's term for murdered, soon after his escape.

As the Soviet Army advanced in 1944, he was transported to another camp, Przemysl, 60 miles west of Lwow to build fortifications. The progress of the Russian forces led to the abandonment of three more camps. The last was made on foot where many of his comrades were shot or beaten to death as they collapsed at the roadside.

At the end of the war he was liberated by British troops in Buchenwald. He remembered the soldiers crying as they encountered the inmates, unable to comprehend the rows of living skeletons lined up behind the barbed wire waving and cheering them. One handsome Major handed him a raw potato, which he ate hungrily. The Major looked surprised. He had expected him to peel it and cook it.

Sick and malnourished he was detained in the camp for months afterwards. He weighed less than eighty pounds and had typhoid. Many continued to die around him.

At the end of 1945, Samuel was sent to a camp for displaced persons run by the British. He discovered there that all his family was dead. Most had been sent to Belzec. It was an extermination camp near Lwow. It had no barracks or workshops. Jews were crushed herring like into cattle trucks, the floors covered in quicklime, which burned through human skin.

Many were dead when the locked doors of the carriages were pulled open at their final destination. The rest were herded straight to the gas chambers. A sick scheme conceived in the minds of lunatics. Sent like cattle to an abattoir to be butchered by men who knew that their crimes were so heinous that extermination orders were never written down. Men too cowardly to put a signature to their actions. Men who were so ashamed that at the time of reckoning they always blamed others.

There were too many bodies to burn. Many were dumped in pits, which were daily covered in a fresh layer of soil and lime. With the problem of disposing of the evidence and the Soviet forces coming ever near, Belzec was abandoned in June 1943. In the fifteen months the camp existed nearly half a million people were murdered by the SS. There were 17 survivors. None were related to Samuel Lebowitz.

During his months of recovery Samuel read in the newspapers about the Nuremberg Trials. A Judgement Day for pitifully few of those that had reduced the world to a living hell.

He read how those mainly responsible – Hitler, Himmler, Goering, Goebbels, Krebs and Burgdorf – had committed suicide. They didn't believe in their cause strongly enough to live to defend it or to martyr themselves in its name. They ran away. They took a route denied to their victims.

The reports called them animals and monsters, but Samuel could think of no other creatures that behaved in this way. What other animal killed its own species or another species en masse? He had seen terrible things in the camps: a man who would sell the life of another for slice of bread. A cat might show more kindness to a mouse. No, such things were the work of men alone. Man was the most dangerous creature that existed; that had ever existed.

Beth was a nurse in the camp. She was from a Jewish family who lived in Glasgow. On hearing of the plight of the victims of the Holocaust she had immediately applied to work in the camps for displaced persons. She had looked after Samuel, still sick and deathly thin, and saw a strong man emerge from an emaciated body.

She told him of Ben Gurion; of the dream of Israel. It became his dream. He had no family to return to in Poland. It seemed nowhere in Europe was safe for his people. Even those who had begun the war fighting the Nazis -the Dutch, the French - had willingly forced their Jewish populations onto trains where the final destination was Auschwitz, Chelmno and Ravensbrueck. Like Beth he came to believe that only a Jewish state could offer sanctuary in a world of anti-Semites.

They married in early 1946. He was issued with a British passport. Samuel was no longer a stateless Jew. Instead of joining the heaving cargoes of Jewish refugees on ships turned away by British gunboats at the ports of Palestine, he and his new wife took a cruise ship to Haifa and entered legally on his new passport in time to witness the birth of a new nation.

Unlike Beth, Samuel did not see the Jews return to Israel as the fulfilling of a prophecy. He no longer believed in any god. If the Holocaust was God's way of gathering in his children from the wilderness then he was clearly insane. Religious pre-destiny may have brought the original Zionists to Palestine but for Samuel it was a haven that might have been there as anywhere else.

In the eyes of the world the word Jew was a stain. A person may never have been near a synagogue or taken part in any of the cultural or religious life of a Jew yet under Nazi law two Jewish grandparents was sufficient qualification for the next cattle train to Auschwitz. Had the Third Reich continued Samuel felt sure that the sieving of the population of Europe would have continued and that any record of mixed blood going back over generations would have resulted in liquidation.

It was not just the Nazis who discriminated. He met Russian Jews in Israel who had been transported thousands of miles under the orders of Stalin. Taken by force from the fertile lands of Georgia and the Ukraine to be dumped in the hostile tundra of Siberia. Ultimately, removed from the invasion of Hitler's hordes it had saved their lives, but it had not been comrade Stalin's intention.

The Soviet state, based on the philosophy of Jews like Marx and Lenin, which preached the brotherhood of man would still stamp on an individual's papers the word "Jew" and take appropriate action. Samuel saw that the problem was the way the world saw him, not the way he saw the world. He was determined though that the next time Jews were attacked they would not die with their hands on their heads. Instead, if they had to die, it would be with their fingers on the triggers of their guns. The lambs of Europe had to become the lions of Judea.

In 1947 the United Nations had voted to partition Palestine to establish a haven for the Jews who had fled there. The land granted to them was less than the state of Connecticut, the third smallest state in the USA.

Samuel sympathised with those Palestinians displaced by this edict but unless the Jews established a new country in Antarctica where were they to go where the status quo would not be disrupted? At least the Jews had settled the land peacefully. Unlike the British, who had tried desperately to keep the Jewish settlers out, they had at least bought the land from the Arabs. Had the British paid the Native Americans, the Aborigines or the Maoris for the lands they settled in America, Canada, Australia or New Zealand?

Samuel saw the birth of his nation but did not live to see the birth of his son. After the declaration of independence in May 1948 the new land was set upon by the armies of five Arab countries, all larger and better equipped, determined to strangle it at birth.

Samuel enlisted in the Haganah, the ragtag paramilitary force that was to become the Israeli army. He was killed by a Jordanian sniper in the first battle of Latrun.

As he lay with his head cradled in a comrade's arms on a cool morning in October staring into a crystal azure sky Samuel was at peace. He had given his life for something when it could so easily have been taken from him for nothing.

When the first Arab-Israeli war ended a year later the new nation had grown to the size of New Jersey, the fourth smallest state in the USA. It was a country that would generate huge controversy in comparison to its diminutive size. In the years to come Arab nations would deflect the problems of their internal dictatorships and oligarchies on its new enemy: Israel. For now, though, Beth and her unborn child were safe, and the dream of a Jewish homeland lived on.

Chapter 8

Simon lived with his mother on the Ruhama kibbutz in the Negev desert. Established in 1911 it was one of the first communal farms. The barren land was bought from the Arabs and over time became bountiful with irrigated field crops and orchards.

Many of the kibbutzniks came before the war: before they Holocaust. They struggled to comprehend the stories of those Jews arriving mainly from Eastern Europe who told tales of being herded into ghettoes and onto trains to be taken and slaughtered in human abattoirs. "Why did you not fight?" was the question they always asked. The survivors of the Holocaust told of the deceit of the Nazis. The lies that they were being taken to work camps or resettled. How they were allowed to pack bags to give them the mistaken hope of a future elsewhere. Of showers that became gas chambers. Others told of resistance: of Treblinka and the Warsaw Ghetto. Still, those who had not lived it did not understand.

Simon learned the story of his father and became determined that pogroms and genocide would never again be the fate of his people. Beth was more circumspect. She ensured her son, like her, held both an Israeli and a British passport. "For a Jew it is important to have somewhere else to go," she would say, although Simon said that he would never leave.

Simon learned many things on the kibbutz. As well as his normal schooling in Hebrew, he spoke English with his mother and learned some German from those who had fled Central and Eastern Europe and whose standard tongue was Yiddish. He learned to farm and grew strong despite being short and wiry.

At the age of 18 in 1966 he was called up by the Israeli Defence Force to do his National Service, a period of two years and eight months. The young men from the Kibbutzs and Moshavs were particularly favoured by the military instructors. They were usually strong and healthy with quick wits from working on the land, and able to work as part of a team.

After finishing his basic training Simon was chosen for a Sayeret Unit. All combat brigades had such a unit with improved weaponry and training for the purpose of reconnaissance and special forces missions. It was considered that such units would often be used behind enemy lines. Emphasis was put on teaching hand-to-hand combat for situations where the use of weapons would give away their presence. The method used was Krav Maga.

Krav Maga, meaning "contact combat" in Hebrew, was developed by Imi Lichtenfeld in the Jewish quarter of Bratislava. Already an accomplished boxer and wrestler he found that these skills did not translate when it came to defending Jewish neighbourhoods from the racist thugs of Slovakia in the 1930s.

On the streets, Lichtenfeld acquired through hard won experience a fundamental understanding of the differences between fighting in a ring and street fighting. On the streets there were no rules, no referees and no bells to begin and end proceedings. Often, a fight was won by the man who made the first move.

Krav Maga was not just self-defence. Equally, it could be used for offensive attack too. It was not a sport or a martial art; it was a system of fighting that borrowed from everywhere and sometimes invented new combat techniques. Its primary aim was for an opponent to be disabled within the first few seconds of any altercation and for any injuries to its proponent to be minimal. It could be used against fists, kicks, bottles, clubs, knives and even guns at close quarters.

Lichtenfeld fled Nazi Europe for Palestine in 1942. The Haganah's leaders immediately recognised his fighting prowess and ingenuity and over the next twenty years he taught them to the elite units of the Israeli Defense Forces, developing and refining the technique. It was in this that Simon Lebowitz was to become expert.

Simon fought in the Six Day War of 1967. He was used as a spotter in the Sinai, identifying Egyptian artillery units to be taken out by the Mirages of the Israeli Air Force. He was made a sergeant in 1968 and, having decided to stay in the army after his National Service was complete, an instructor of Krav Maga.

Simon was at home watching the television news on a September morning in 1972. The breathless report coming from the Olympic Village in Munich. He saw the body of a dead Israeli athlete lying in a heap in front of a door.

The news reporter said a group of Palestinians, the Black September Group, were demanding the release of 234 Palestinians jailed in Israel. They also demanded the release of Andreas Baader and Ulrike Meinhoff from prison in West Germany. These two Germans claimed to represent the radical left, but their hatred of Jews was the same as Himmler's or Heydrich's. As with all ideologies, the theory often overwhelmed the humanity.

Over the next two days the crisis played out culminating in the bungled rescue attempt by West

German police at Furstenfeldbruck airfield. All the hostages were massacred by the Black September group. Simon watched the report from the American network ABC:

"We have just got the final word… You know, when I was a kid, my father used to say: "Our greatest hopes and our worst fears are seldom realized." Our worst fears have been realized tonight. They've now said that there were eleven hostages. Two were killed in their rooms yesterday morning, nine were killed at the airport tonight. They're all gone."

He watched as the newsreader struggled to control his grief. Simon cried. He cried again with many others when he joined the crowd at Lod Airport as the coffins were returned home with the Israeli Olympic team.

The bodies of the five Palestinian attackers killed at Furstenfeldbruck were delivered to Libya, where they received heroes' funerals and were buried with full military honours. The three members of the Black September group who had survived the attack, were held in custody awaiting trial by the West German police.

The 1972 Olympic Games were not cancelled in the aftermath of the massacre. Only Israel withdrew from the competition. The Germans seemed to wish to forget the events that had happened on their soil as they had 27 years before. Eventually, after much criticism, it was decided to suspend the games for a day. At the memorial service the President of the International Olympic Committee gave a speech. He made little reference to the murders. The flags of all the competing nations were flown at half-mast except for ten Arab nations who insisted that their nation's emblems were flown at the top of the flagpoles.

A few weeks later Lufthansa Flight 615 from Damascus was hijacked; there was a threat that the airplane would be blown up if the Munich attackers were not released. The West German authorities complied, and the three surviving Black September members were handed over at Zargreb airport, and the hijacked aircraft was flown to Tripoli to the rapturous welcome of Muammar Gaddafi and the Libyan people.

Simon suspected that this had been convenient. By this time, he was working with Mossad, the Israeli intelligence service. When he spoke to his friends in Mossad, they shared his suspicions. Flight 615 had a seating capacity of 130 and yet there were only 13 passengers on board. The surprisingly quick decision to release the prisoners supported the theory that West Germany simply wished to wash its hands of the problem and had acted in tandem with the Black September group. Later interviews and confessions gave credence to this theory.

Simon realized once again that his mother was right. The only country in the world where it was safe to be a Jew was Israel. Even if nations were not directly responsible for the continuing discrimination and murder of the Jews, they continued to be complicit in it.

Following the massacre of Israel's athletes, the Prime Minister, Golda Meir, launched operation Wrath of God to take her revenge on the Black September group. Simon became involved with the assassins who would extract their revenge in shootings on the streets of Rome and Paris. Two more targets were blown up by bombs planted in their rooms, and another was pushed under a bus in London.

Mossad were already trained in Krav Maga, but these reprisal attacks could not be directly attributable to Israel, so it was important that these skills were honed and used against opponents who were also trained in hand to hand combat.

At night, after dinner in their training camp the agents of Mossad would discuss their fieldcraft with Simon: how to do background checks using public records, how to tail a man without being spotted, and how to pick locks on cars and buildings. In those few short weeks Simon felt that he had gained as much knowledge as he had imparted. He also realized that an army did not simply depend on strength alone. The gathering and use of intelligence was equally important, and Mossad were the best in the world at that.

In 1973 the Arab armies again tried to wipe Israel from the map. Simon fought on the Golan Heights. For the first two days the battle was desperate with Syrian tanks driving deep into Israeli territory. By the third day the army was remobilized and began to push back the enemy. Within a week Israeli artillery was shelling Damascus. Simon was not there to see it. He had been wounded in the leg by a shell fragment and was recovering in a field hospital. His leg eventually healed but not sufficiently to continue his role as a combat instructor. He decided to retire from the army.

During his time in the military he had learned many things: mountaineering, sailing, ski-ing and, best of all, scuba diving. Having given nearly ten years of devoted service to his country, Simon now decided that he would look for a job where he could indulge his aquatic passion. The southern town of Eilat, which was situated on the northern tip of the Red Sea, had started to develop as a tourist destination. Simon quickly found work there, teaching and leading scuba expeditions on the resort's wonderful reefs during the day and working as a hotel barman at night.

Eilat had visitors from many countries. One night whilst working at the bar of a hotel in the town he served three men. They were smartly dressed and appeared to be in their late 50s or early 60s. It was winter so many international companies held conferences in the resort at this time of year. They ordered their drinks in English but spoke German amongst themselves.

It was a Friday and Simon wore his kippah with a Star of David embroidered on the crown. He was not listening to their conversation but heard the word "Juden" repeatedly. He caught their sidelong glances and low, conspiratorial laughter. The men were drunk, and leery, as often business guests were.

Simon was the late-night concierge. There was little scuba work to be had in the colder months. His role was to deal with any guest issues and to provide a basic room service, drinks and sandwiches, for people in the small hours when the bar and restaurant was closed. It was twenty minutes after midnight. The telephone rang on his desk and a man in room 121 asked for a large whisky and soda to be brought up.

Five minutes later he was knocking at the door of the room with a tray in his hand. The door was answered by one of the German men. He held the door open and gestured towards a table where he should place the tray. The man did not speak. Simon entered the room. It was dim, lit only by a lamp on the bedside table. He did not see the discarded shoes in the middle of the floor. As he tripped the tumbler of whisky and jug of soda water slipped sideways off the tray soaking the hotel guest who was still holding the door open.

Simon grabbed a cloth napkin and mumbled his apologies as his dabbed at the man's wet shirt. Then he felt a stinging blow. "Get your hands off me you fucking Jew!" he shouted. Simon stepped back. He was flustered. The man looked at his name badge. "Lebowitz," he said slowly and mimed tattooing a number onto the inside of his left arm. "Belzec for you, Lebowitz."

As a combat instructor, he always taught people to try and fight unemotionally. Adrenaline often confounded logic. An exponent of Krav Maga should be as cool as a chess master looking to deliver checkmate in two moves. His training and conditioning counted for nothing this time. His anger erupted like a volcano. He hit the man. A straight punch delivered to the nose and the mouth. He felt bones crack and teeth give way. The man fell backward hitting his head on the edge of the door.

Simon knelt next to the prone figure. He heard a rattle in the man's throat. He put his ear next to the man's mouth. He could not feel breathing. Simon pushed on the man's chest stopping to hold his nose and breath into his mouth.

The man's breath stank: Simon retched. He pulled open the man's shirt, the better to locate his heart, and noticed a mottled scar by his left armpit. Simon had read that for authorities seeking to bring former Nazis to trial for war crimes this was an identifying mark they looked for. All SS personnel had been required to have a blood group tattoo on that part of their body. After the war, attempting to remove such a revelatory piece of evidence, most opted to burn it off. Simon stopped trying to resuscitate the man.

He pulled the body into the room and closed the door. He thought about his predicament. He only had a few hours before the dead man was discovered. The police would inevitably ask questions. There was blood and smashed teeth spread around. Had the punch killed him or had it brought on a heart attack or seizure? Simon did not know. Whatever, if the blame came back to him this was manslaughter at the least. A long prison sentence, even with extenuating circumstances. He was a trained combat instructor too. Any prosecutor would claim that he knew what he was doing. Perhaps, on that basis you could argue that it was second-degree murder?

Simon decided that it would be better for him to disappear. He rebuttoned the man's shirt but left him lying where he was. Maybe if it was a heart attack then his other injuries could be attributed to the fall? He picked up the tray and whisky glass and returned them to the kitchen, washing them carefully in the sink. Then he went to his room. As a soldier all his clothes were tidily folded into the drawers of a dresser. He transferred them into two soft holdalls. Finally, he took his two passports from the bedside drawer. The Israeli passport he hid in his washbag. The British one he put in his shirt pocket.

Chapter 9

Eilat is right on the border with Jordan. Although they had not participated in the Yom Kippur War the Jordanians begrudged the territory Israel had taken from them in 1967 and effectively the border was closed to citizens of the Jewish state. It remained open to allow goods shipped into the port of Aqaba to be transported into Israel and for the free movement of tourists holidaying in the Red Sea resorts.

There were superb diving sites near Aqaba, and Simon had been keen to take guests there. Many also wanted to see the wonders of Petra, Wadi Rum, Jaresh and the Dead Sea, which were all just a few hours' drive from the border. For this reason, Simon had obtained a tourist visa to Jordan using his British passport. It was something that he renewed as soon as the old one expired, so that it was always current. It was a piece of luck, which was vital in his escape.

Within twenty minutes Simon, seated in his Fiat 500, was handing his British passport to the Jordanian soldier at the border, who looked at the visa and waved him through. An hour later he was at Aqaba airport and three hours after that he was on a flight to London.

When he arrived at Heathrow airport Simon knew that the trail had to go cold from there. Before crossing the border into Jordan, he had stopped at a cash machine in Eilat and managed to obtain a few hundred shekels from his account. He paid for his air ticket using a credit card. Anybody wishing to speak to him about the murder of an elderly German businessman could trace him this far. But London was a city of eight million souls. They would need to know where to look and besides, he did not plan to stay in London. His mother, Beth, had died in 1978 but Simon still had family in Glasgow, where she was originally from. He had an address and he planned to head there.

In 1973, during the Yom Kippur War, a great many Jews had travelled to Israel to help protect the nation against the surprise onslaught of the Arab armies. The day had been a national holiday when armies from Egypt in the West and Syria in the East invaded, intending to squeeze Israel in a vice.

The struggle was desperate, and the help of the Diaspora was sought and welcomed. Amongst them was David Katz, Simon's cousin. They had served together on the Syrian border and David had looked after his cousin after he was wounded. David had eventually returned to Britain, but in the following years he had visited Simon in Eilat for snorkelling holidays. There would always be a warm welcome for his cousin in Scotland.

Simon changed his shekels for British pounds at the airport and bought a cheap coach ticket to the bus station in central Glasgow. After a long and boring journey lasting over eight hours, he finally stepped down from the coach that now stank of fast food, bad breath and sweat. There was a red telephone box right outside and he called his cousin.

Half an hour later, David picked him up in a beaten-up Volvo. Simon explained his predicament as he was driven to his cousin's rented flat in Paisley.

The two men talked deep into the night. They decided that it would be better if there were no official records of Simon's whereabouts. Registering for work or unemployment benefit would lead investigators straight to him. The dilemma was that he had only enough money to last him for a few days at best. Yes, he had a credit card but using it would reveal his location and he was too proud to live on the charity of his relatives.

David owned a small Jewish bakery in a quiet side street in the Gorbals. He had inherited it from his now deceased parents. When the shop was established in the 1930s it catered for the thriving Jewish community supplying the Challah bread, bagels and apple cakes for Friday night dinners, Jewish holidays, weddings and Bar Mitzvahs.

As the community became better off and less orthodox they moved to the more affluent neighbourhoods in the south of Glasgow or emigrated to America. By the time David took over the business was struggling. He had let three of the staff go and now ran the business by himself with just part-time help. Getting up in the middle of the night to bake left him with almost no social life and working as a solitary employee was lonely. It was decided Simon could work there. That way there would be no official records. David would pay him cash and provide his cousin with accommodation in the spare bedroom of his flat. It was an arrangement that suited them both.

Simon did not like the Gorbals. It lacked the warmth and space of the Negev and the Red Sea. He felt that he was back in the ghetto that his father had eventually escaped from. The Jews who still lived here were orthodox. The men dressed in black with large hats and ringlets, the women with shaven heads and wigs. Most were Haredi Jews. They did not believe in Israel and those back in his homeland refused to do National Service. The men and women were strictly segregated, whereas Simon had fought alongside women soldiers in the army and worked shoulder to shoulder with them in the fields of the kibbutz.

Before he left Israel, Simon had read in the newspapers that these orthodox Jews had started settling in the West Bank, a situation to which the government was opposed. It was paradoxical that they did not believe in Israel, would not fight in its army and yet tried to settle in a buffer zone established after the Six Day War. They created problems for the nation and yet contributed nothing towards it.

Although David did not have ringlets he dressed traditionally when at work. Simon knew that he was not orthodox and when he asked him why he wore the costume of the Polish ghetto his cousin shrugged and said, "these people are my customers."

Simon mainly worked in the back of the shop, baking. He missed the heat of the desert and the room with its hot oven was the only place he ever felt properly warm. Besides, the customers did not want to be served by a man that looked like a goy.

Friday was the busiest day. The two cousins would rise two hours early to make enough cakes and bread. By midday they had always sold out and David would walk with his takings to the bank before coming back to the shop to close up and drive Simon home.

As he waited for David to return, Simon would often notice from his seat at the back of the shop two men waiting outside. They were not Jews, at least not traditional ones. They wore leather jackets, jeans and training shoes.

When David returned, he would always stand outside talking to the two men before handing them an envelope. It looked like it contained banknotes. Simon wondered if they were the shop's landlords, but his cousin had told him that he owned the shop. Maybe the premises were leasehold, and he was paying the ground rent? Although collecting it weekly in such large sums did not seem to make sense. When Simon asked about the men, David was always quick to change the subject.

One Friday, just before the feast of the Passover, one of the biggest holidays, the bakery had been busy all day. The two men had worked all night and baked twice as much as they would do normally. Despite this they had still sold out of everything by 11 o'clock that morning.

David had gone to the bank early. Simon sat in the back room drinking coffee and awaiting the return of his cousin. He had been reading a newspaper and listening to classical music on the radio. He was surprised to hear the shop bell ring. He looked up to see David panting and dishevelled. He looked close to tears. Simon led him into the back room and gave him his seat. "I've been robbed," he gasped, half panting, half sobbing. He explained that two men had held him at knifepoint and made away with the bag of money. "It was almost two thousand pounds!" he said.

A movement in the shop window caught Simon's eye. It was the two men in leather jackets. "Was it them?" he shouted, pointing towards them. The men heard and stared back at him. "No, no," said David standing up and pushing his cousin towards the empty chair. "It wasn't them. Leave them to me. I need to speak to them." He exited the shop.

Simon watched the exchange from his seat. David was taking fast, the palms of his hands held out in a placatory gesture. The men looked angry, he could hear their raised voices, but he could not hear the words. One of them pushed David hard in the chest.

Simon got up and walked quickly towards the shop door. As he stepped into the street the two men stopped shouting and stared at him. "Who the fuck are you?" asked one. "Simon, go back in the shop. Leave it," pleaded David.

"Yes Simon, fuck off," said the other man and stepped towards him pulling his right fist back. Simon stepped to his left around the man, grabbed his arm by the wrist and, still moving, drew it up into the small of the man's back. The man gave a shout. "Walk away my friend," he whispered into the man's ear.

He looked up to see that the other man had pulled a knife. It was a long Sabatier type, the sort chef's used in professional kitchens. As a combat instructor, his advice was always to run when somebody pulled a knife. There was no shame in a tactical retreat when your enemy had the advantage. And knives were unpredictable: far more so than guns. Unless it was at close range, there was a good chance of a gunshot missing.

Most people could not really handle firearms. He had fought Arabs with Kalashnikovs. Despite being able to fire 10 rounds per second they often missed everything, firing high or wide. Guns took special training, they needed to be looked after: cleaned and oiled. At close quarters, any idiot with a knife could inflict fatal damage. But David was there, clasping his hands together agitatedly. If he ran, he was sure that David would not see tomorrow.

Simon twisted the man's hand through an arc, he felt the arm dislocate from the shoulder socket and the limb go lose. He let go and pushed his crying opponent towards the man with the knife.

The man held the knife in his right-hand, so Simon moved to his opponents left side and punched the man in the ear. He kept moving, faster than the man who was trying to swivel round. He was behind his adversary. He grabbed the man's wrist with his right hand with an overhand grip and under the man's elbow with his left hand at the same time, neutralising the attacking limb. He pulled the wrist down and pushed the elbow joint up rupturing it. The man screamed, and the knife clattered on the pavement as it fell from his hand.

For a moment there was silence. The first man grabbed the second by the collar with his good hand and they moved away in a slinking run. Simon could not help but thing of Charles Laughton in the Hunchback of Notre Dame.

As they turned the corner, the first one shouted "You're both dead and your shop will be in flames by the morning."

Simon began to run towards them. He could hear his cousin shouting at him to stop. He turned the corner and caught up with the two men. He grabbed the first one by the collar and smashed his face into a brick wall. He felt the man's body go limp under him. He let go. He turned to the second man who was crouched down supporting the weight of his body with his good arm. The man stared up at him with hatred in his eyes, like a trapped rat. "If I see either of you again, I will kill you both." The man nodded. Simon kicked his supporting arm away and the man gasped.

Simon went back to the shop where he telephoned an ambulance, giving the address of the next street and explaining that two men had been in a motorcycle accident. He knew the police rarely attended traffic accidents unless they were fatal.

David was pestering him for them both to leave. As they drove home, he explained that he had always had to pay protection money, as did every other shopkeeper and business owner in the area.

"But you were robbed. Where was their protection when that happened?" asked Simon.

David shook his head sadly at his cousin's naivety. "It doesn't work like that. You pay money to them so that they don't attack you. Unfortunately, I didn't have anything to give them, the robbers took it all."

"Thank you for intervening but it would have been better if you hadn't. These are very dangerous men. We can't go back to the shop. In fact, it would be better if we went straight home, packed and left Glasgow altogether. Our lives are in danger."

Simon could see that David was scared. He agreed to leave Glasgow. When they got back to the flat, they packed holdalls and were gone within ten minutes.

David drove to the house of his uncle Jim, in Kirkcaldy. He explained that a waterpipe had burst at his flat and that they needed somewhere to stay for a few days. Jim, who lived alone, was more than welcoming.

Over the next few days David's agitation grow worse. "Where I am to go now?" he would ask. "I have nowhere to live and no job. I will have to start all over again." Simon felt guilty. He had tried to do what was best but the road to hell is paved with good intentions.

After a few days, Simon had made up his mind. He had run away from Israel, and now he was running away from Glasgow. He decided to go back. He thought of the words of the ABC news reporter: "Our greatest hopes and our worst fears are seldom realized."

He would go back to the flat and back to the shop. The worst they could do was kill him and that was a fear that he had faced before in the Sinai and on the Golan Heights. He told David to stay with Jim and that if he was not in touch in a week for his cousin to seek a new life elsewhere.

Chapter 10

Simon sat in the Volvo, which was parked in a side street with a view of the flat. After six hours he decided that nobody was watching the building.

He went inside and opened the front door. There was no sign that the place had been broken into. He taped up the letterbox and sealed the bottom of the front door so that petrol could not be poured through and then set alight. He made himself ready for an early start the next morning.

He arrived at 5 a.m. Like the flat, the shop was still standing. The steel shutter was still pulled down over the front of the shop. If anybody had been there, they certainly had not tried to gain access or burn the place down.

He went into the back, lit the oven and tuned the radio to BBC Radio 4. He scooped the flour and butter into the giant mechanical mixer and added water. The bread was ready by 6 a.m. and the cakes soon after. As usual, they sold out. Nothing else happened, and he went home.

Three more days elapsed. Still nothing happened. Simon was beginning to think that the two men who operated the protection racket were not connected in the way they had told David that they were. Maybe they were not part of a gang? In which case there was just the two of them and both would still be in slings and plaster casts. They would not be coming back, he thought.

Simon was cleaning up in the kitchen, making ready for the next day's baking. It was a job that suited a soldier.

The machinery had to be dry, polished and lubricated, just like a rifle. The floors and surfaces had to be scrubbed clean and the utensils washed and placed neatly away, just like a barracks. He was listening to a play on the radio. It was as important to feed your head as your body, he thought.

The bell rang as the shop door opened. Simon peered from the kitchen at a man who stood at the counter. He was not a typical customer. He had an expensive camel coat on and a tie: the Haredi Jews always wore black and never wore ties. "I'm sorry, but we are closed. We have sold everything," he said and gestured with his hand at the empty shelves.

"I have nae come to buy anything," said the man, his Glasgow accent broad and harsh. "I understand that there was a wee fracas here last week?"

"I don't know anything about it," Simon shook his head. "Are you the police?"

"Oh, no," the man smiled as if he had been told a joke. He looked towards the back room. "Would you mind if we talked in there?" he gestured with his head.

Simon lifted the flap on the counter that gave access to the back of the shop. He walked to the door and turned the sign from "Open" to "Closed." He flipped the snib deadlock and drew the bolt and flicked his eyes from side to side. The street was empty. He turned and ushered the man into the back. He switched off the radio.

"Arthur Wilson, good to see you," said the man extending his hand.

"Simon Lebowitz. What can I do for you?" he said shaking the man's hand briefly and pushing a stool towards his visitor. The man sat down.

"Two of my boys have been in the hospital," he began. Simon began to shake his head and look surprised but before he could speak Arthur Wilson waved his hand for silence. "No, no, don't argue. I know it was you." He was quiet for a moment. "Very impressive too. They said you seemed like a professional" he smiled. "Did you learn that in the army?"

Simon nodded.

"Which regiment? Some hairy-arsed bastards I bet? The Paras or the Marines?"

Simon shook his head. "The Israeli army. I was a combat instructor."

Arthur gave a low whistle. "Oh fuck, my two bairns stood no chance then. Are you new, they said they had never seen you before?"

"Yes, this place is owned by my cousin David. I started a few weeks ago."

"And where is David?" Arthur asked.

"He's gone away. He's too frightened to come back."

Arthur nodded. "Aye, sensible laddie. Listen, I cannae say I'm happy about what happened but the two that you put in the hospital are just small fry, they will do what I tell them. As I said, I am very impressed. Even more so now that you have told me that you were in the Israeli army. How long was that for?"

"Eight years," said Simon coldly.

"In my business I find it very difficult to find men like you. Capable men. I can find lots of hot heads. Kids full of piss and vinegar. They do a reasonable enough job and are easy to replace if they fuck up. Parts of my operation need a more considered approach though. Somebody more mature and intelligent." He pointed at the radio. "Someone who listens to Radio 4 like me, not all that boom- boom, bash-bash nigger music."

Arthur stretched his legs out and folded his arms. "What I am saying, is that you need to come and work for me. The deal is that you would be a lot better off, I need guys like you and I am happy to pay for it. Your cousin gets his life back and gets to keep his shop and he won't have to pay my gorillas every week."

Simon looked thoughtful. "No. I don't want to rob people. I'm not leaning on people like my cousin."

Arthur smiled coldly. "And you have principles too. I like that even more. Somebody I can trust. Let me start by saying that the alternative is pretty bleak. You and your cousin wouldn't just have to get out of Glasgow, you would have to leave the country to be safe, and even then..." he trailed off.

Again, he was quiet, considering what he was about to say. "Listen, I don't like protection rackets either. You're right; we are taking money off the wrong people. They are old school, something that I inherited. What I need you for is something that is far more lucrative. A product which people will willingly pay for."

"Drugs?" said Simon.

Arthur nodded. "I imagine that is against your principles as well. I understand. Booze is my weakness. And yet, in the 1920s in America that was illegal too, and yet people couldn't get enough of it. Drugs are the same. One day, it will all be legal. It's a war that the authorities can't win. What I sell though is only to consenting adults, not to kids. The tobacco companies are more cynical than I am. In 20 years, cannabis will be legal, and cigarettes won't."

"So, it's just cannabis?" asked Simon.

"Yes," Arthur lied. He figured that once this man understood the extent of his drugs empire, he would have blood on his hands, both metaphorically and literally, and it would be too late to turn back.

"I am not asking you to deal it. I just need you to back me up. To check out venues where I am meeting up with suppliers. To be my security really, and your military training will really help with that," said Arthur.

In this respect, he told the truth. Cocaine was becoming the drug de jour, and its main source was the 'Ndrangheta, the mafia gang based in Calabria in the toe of Italy. Through the proceeds from kidnapping, in particular of John Paul Getty's grandson, they had subsidised the building of a deep-water port, Gioia Tauro. It was becoming the largest container port in the country and 80% of the cocaine in Europe moved through it.

The 'Ndrangheta had established a huge wholesale supply network across the Continent. Arthur was the local retailer in Glasgow. He was buying his supplies from a gang, which had come seemingly from nowhere. All he knew was they had the reputation for tremendous violence and who would potentially move in on his operation if he was unable to defend his territory. The police too were becoming more sophisticated in the methods they used to break criminal gangs. He needed the intelligence and counter intelligence skills of men like Simon.

Simon rocked back and forth on his stool as he considered his options. He did not want Arthur to know about the possibility of being sought to stand trial for murder by the Israeli police. Already the man had enough leverage over him, if he knew this he would be at his mercy. "Listen, I'm illegal in this country. I can't show up on any employment records or anything."

"Even better," said Arthur.

"There is one final thing," said Simon. Arthur smiled and raised his eyebrows. This man had his back to the wall and was still fighting. He liked that. "Your men were supposed to protect my cousin's shop. They didn't. Instead they allowed him to be robbed and still expected him to pay. If you want me to work for you then you should pay him back all the protection money you have ever taken from him."

Arthur felt like laughing. The man had balls of steel. "Agreed," he said and rose to shake Simon's hand.

And so, Simon Lebowitz came to work for Arthur Wilson. The job was much as described. Initially, Simon never saw or handled drugs. His main role was surveillance on other gangs and on the Italians, who supplied Arthur's organization.

His close work with Mossad when he was in the army had taught him many useful techniques. He would observe venues for arranged meeting days and sometimes weeks in advance. Often the work was boring, simply sitting and observing the comings and goings from a house, a pub or an hotel. His counter surveillance training meant he could search a room very quickly for hidden listening devices and weapons. He was equally proficient in searching a man, and spotting from a distance anybody who was carrying a weapon.

Simon checked Arthur's home and work premises for bugs too, as he did for any of the main man's accomplices and associates. He also advised on personal security. He set up cameras and monitors, established safe rooms and escape routes and advised on the construction of sophisticated hiding places for weapons or drugs. He also did deep background checks into all gang members and any associates, spending days at Somerset House obtaining birth certificates and then ordering death certificates to see if an identity had been borrowed from an expired host.

Surprisingly, he identified the weak point in Arthur's security as being his son, Arthur Junior, or Fatboy as he was known behind the boy's and his father's backs. On looking into the background of Fatboy's friends it became obvious that two of them were police informers and one was somebody that officially did not exist, either planted by the police or a rival gang. Arthur Junior was also a loud mouth. He would boast about the gang's criminal enterprises and be quite happy to tell a stranger how an operation or scam worked when he was drunk, which was most of the time.

When Simon shared his findings to Arthur, Fatboy was called into the office. He had a look of hatred in his eyes as three of his friends were revealed to be Judases. As Simon made his way down the stairs, he could hear the invective and expletives the older man poured upon his useless son. Undoubtedly, steps would be taken straight away to ensure the silence of the traitors. Simon knew he had made an enemy in Fatboy and that he would not be forgiven.

A few months later, Simon was called into Arthur's office. He was told that there had been a tip off that the port of Glasgow was being watched very thoroughly by the Drugs Squad and that they planned to make a series of raids on the container ships that usually smuggled consignments of cocaine into the city. Arthur had decided to postpone the normal method of delivery. Instead, he arranged with the 'Ndrangheta to transport the goods by fishing vessels coming from

Holland. These boats would never dock but would simply unload their illegal cargo onto fast motor launches. The goods would then be transported to remote beaches to be loaded into cars and vans and taken to safe houses in the city. Simon had mentioned one day that he was a snorkelling instructor back in Israel and Arthur had remembered it. He was required to operate one of the motor launches.

It was pure bad luck that Simon was caught by the Coast Guard. The runs were made at night, and the launch was always in complete darkness. He heard the Cutter's engine before he saw it, but it seemed to be able to follow his path no matter how he zig-zagged across the sea. He thought perhaps the chasing vessel was equipped with some type of very sophisticated radar. It was clear that he was not going to outrun his pursuers and dumped the packages of drugs into the ocean.

Eventually, the Cutter shone a high beam on his launch and ordered him to cut his engine. He had prepared himself for such an eventuality and brought five thousand cigarettes on each of his runs. They were cigarettes that Arthur had already smuggled into Scotland. He reasoned that if he was stopped it would look like he was smuggling cigarettes and the prison sentence was likely to be much shorter than being caught with Class A drugs.

This was how Simon Lebowitz found himself serving twenty-six months in Barlinnie Gaol and how he came to be sharing a cell with Jaimie McGovern.

Chapter 11

Life became much easier when it became known throughout Barlinnie that Jaimie McGovern was protected by Simon Lebowitz, and by extension Arthur Wilson's gang. The nonces who had made his initial weeks in prison lonely and frightening avoided him, preferring to stop and turn around than walk past him in a corridor. Jaimie took his revenge. He would deliberately target them in the mess hall and in the exercise yard making them move away as soon as he approached them.

Jaimie and Simon became ever closer. At first, the older man would simply dispense advice, warning him who to be wary of. Gradually, the conversations would become longer. The young man would sit enthralled by his cellmate's tales of life in the Israeli army. Jaimie knew very little of the world. He had only ever heard of Israel in the lyrics of the hymns he sang at the church he was made to attend every Sunday when he lived in the children's home. All the adults spoke of Heaven and love and yet delivered neglect, abuse and cruelty.

Simon was the first man who had ever paid attention to him. Together they would listen to a radio programme or a piece of music and then sit and discuss it. Jaimie felt for the first time that better possibilities might exist for him. Despite being locked in a cell, which was twelve feet by eight for twenty-three hours a day, for the first time in his life he felt happy. As Simon often said: "Four walls does not a prison make."

For the first few weeks, Jaimie would watch idly from his bed as his cellmate performed an extensive programme of exercise every day. It would start with a series of stretches, then press ups and sit ups, then weight and resistance training using a tin of beans as hand weights and the bars on the cell window for pull-ups. Finally, Simon would sit cross-legged on the floor and go into a trance. Jaimie quickly understood that he should remain very quiet for this part of his friend's regime. If he made a noise Simon would open one eye and angrily stare at him.

Eventually, Jaimie began to join in. He realized that the older man was in much better shape than him. At first, Jaimie could only manage a few press-ups and sit-ups before collapsing into a panting heap and the pull-ups were beyond him. Simon could do the exercises with ease. But Jaimie was young, and his body adapted quickly. Within a few weeks he was able to keep pace with his cellmate. He noticed that the hours passed more quickly too and that he fell asleep as soon as the screws turned off the cell's light.

As the young man's fitness improved, Simon began to incorporate Krav Maga into the programme. It was almost impossible to practice the discipline alone, and he had become rusty. He needed a training partner, and Jaimie was enthusiastic to learn. He demonstrated the weak areas down the front of the body to start; a hard stamp to the ankle, a kick through the knee, an open-handed slap to the balls, a short punch to the solar plexus, a finger push on the windpipe, a straight-handed upward push to the nose and an eye gouge with fingers. Some were intended as "soft stops": something that would temporarily disable an opponent but do no lasting damage like a blow to the balls. Some would mean a trip to the hospital. Some would kill.

Next came the use of locks and chokes. How to maintain them when you were applying them and how to get out of them when you were not.

As the training continued, Simon demonstrated techniques borrowed from Thai boxing: of using elbows rather than fists to strike at short distances, something a prison cell was ideally suited for, and using kicks to strike at a range beyond your opponent's fist. Finally, he introduced Brazilian Ju Jitsu: a discipline that gives its exponent the ability to fight and recover after being wrestled, punched or kicked to the ground.

Jaimie learned that in a fight size, power and aggression were all things that could be countered. By the time Simon was released from Barlinnie ten months later Jaimie McGovern was fit, hard muscled, disciplined and able to look after himself. The two men embraced as the screw unlocked the cell door. Simon had become a father figure to Jaimie and the younger man promised to seek him out as soon as he was released himself.

Fourteen weeks later, as Jaimie walked through the gates of Barlinnie Simon was standing waiting for him. They had kept in touch though visits, letters and telephone calls. Simon said that he had a job lined up for his young friend.

As Arthur Wilson had grown older, and his health began to decline he had shifted more responsibility for the day to day running of his crime empire on his son, Arthur Junior, or Fatboy as everybody else called him.

Simon had never liked Fatboy. He considered him to be out of control. He over ate, he drank far too much, and, although his father did not know, he used cocaine. A lot of cocaine. The boy entirely relied on his father's reputation to maintain his position. Simon convinced Arthur that Fatboy needed a guiding hand and had lined Jaimie McGovern up for that role: somebody clean, sober and disciplined and who would feed news back of any misdemeanours.

In the car on the way to meet Arthur, he stressed to his young friend that it was important that Fatboy did not know of their connection. Fatboy hated Simon. Instead, Jaimie was to be introduced as a new minder to the heir apparent. The story was that Arthur had talent spotted Jaimie in one of his nightclubs taking on three sailors and winning. Simon looked at his young friend; it was not so very far from the truth. He was fit, well-trained and ruthless. Somebody who could shepherd Arthur's idiot son through the mean streets of Glasgow without too much harm coming to him.

Initially, Jaimie got on fine with Fatboy. They would go to clubs and parties. It was fun after being in jail for nearly two years. He would use the excuse that he was driving to get around having to indulge in the ever-available booze and drugs; something to which his charge helped himself freely. At the end of most evenings, he would drive Fatboy home, help him into his house, up the stairs and put him to bed.

All too often though, Jaimie would have to extract Fatboy from a tense situation. Arthur Junior was free with his mouth and seemed to love to rile people. Usually, a quiet word from Jaimie was enough to resolve tensions but there had been two occasions where he had resorted to violence. When Fatboy saw what his new friend could do it made him worse. Not only could he hide behind his father's reputation he now had a pet rottweiler on hand. At that point Jaimie came to despise him, although he kept it well hidden.

Away from the gang, Simon and Jaimie saw each other regularly. They now had their work as a common interest and discussed the various players and schemes that they were involved in. Jaimie told his mentor of the problems that he had with Fatboy. Simon would shake his head. "He hates you, you know?" Jaimie warned. "I know," said Simon nodding, "but while his father is around, I am safe."

They continued to practice Krav Maga a few times every week. Now not confined to the regime of a prison Simon showed his apprentice defences against attacks with bat and snooker cues and how to disarm a man with a knife or a gun. He also showed Jaimie how to handle a gun. The way to hold it when firing. The way to strip, clean and oil it.

From his training with Mossad Simon also showed Jaimie how to steal cars and break into buildings plus fieldcraft of how to observe a man without him knowing. At Simon's suggestion, Jaimie now had his clothes custom made. The shoes had steel tipped heels to inflict maximum damage. The toecaps were steel too, for attack and defence. His suits were hand cut, to disguise the bulge under the armpit that a gun made.

One day, as Simon sat with his young friend stripping and cleaning their guns, he looked up. "I hope one day that we won't need to do this anymore," he said.

After being arrested for tobacco smuggling and sent to Barlinnie, Simon had realized that there had been no enquiry about killing the German man in Eilat. The Israeli police would have been able to track him to the UK and If they had this surely would have shown up on the records of the British police when he was arrested? He thought the Israeli police must have come to a different conclusion: that it was a heart attack, or the man had fallen and hit his head when he was drunk.

Simon hated Glasgow. The stinking weather. The pale, under-nourished angry people. He decided he would save some money and return home. He spoke to Jaimie about it. He wanted to come too. They both conceived of a new start in the warm, desert sun. "I'll go first. If the coast is clear I will let you know, then you can join me," he said. Jaimie applied for a passport.

With Arthur Senior on the scene, there was only so much trouble that Fatboy could get into before his father reigned him in. He would stare sullenly at Simon as his father dressed him down, wondering where he got his information from? All this was to change.

When Arthur Senior had his first stroke, he could give no instructions. He could not speak at first, and it took months of therapy before he was able to work again. This was Fatboy's opportunity to take over the running of the organization. Things very quickly fell apart. Arthur Senior had a good relationship with the 'Ndrangheta. The product was good, and he always paid on time. If any consignments were picked up by the police or the customs' men they were always happy to split the cost.

Fatboy felt that he could get a better deal. He argued with the Calabrians about the price of the cocaine they were supplying. He also approached the Central American cartels about buying the goods directly from them and cutting out the Mafia middlemen. The 'Ndrangheta came to know about this and the once exclusive deal Arthur had with them in Scotland was abandoned. In an act of revenge, they started supplying the Albanian gangs in Glasgow as well and put the price of the product up for Fatboy.

Arthur Junior's retribution was to withhold payment for the next consignment of cocaine that he received. The 'Ndrangheta chased for the repayment for weeks, but Fatboy ignored their requests. Eventually, they sent him a final demand: a goat's head in the post with a note that simply said: "pay by Monday."

The total amount owed was four hundred thousand pounds, but the price had been increased by the Italians by ten per cent for Fatboy's disloyalty. In Arthur Junior's eyes, he only owed three hundred and sixty thousand pounds. This was the amount he put in the bag for Simon to take. He did not bother to tell his delivery man this.

Simon's body was found on the street the next morning. He had been shot from behind, through the throat. His hands had been severed, the Calabrian Mafia's sign for a thief. When Jaimie heard he went home and cried. It was the first time that he had ever shed a tear for anything or anyone. He poured himself a whisky and cut and sniffed a line of coke. It was something that would fill the void in his soul for a while. For the next few months this was to become his daily habit. When he accompanied Fatboy to a club he no longer sat sipping a coke. He now joined in. It was the only peace he could find.

Simon's funeral was small. It was held at a synagogue in central Glasgow. Jaimie attended along with Simon's cousin and his uncle. Nobody else came. Fatboy sent a wreath. He did not seem to care. No steps had been taken to find out the circumstances of his death. He began to feel that Arthur Junior was in some way complicit, but he could not identify how.

On the streets, things were getting out of hand. With no supplies coming from the 'Ndrangheta they were having to source cocaine from elsewhere and then cut it with laxative or milk powder to string out their dwindling access to the product. Other gangs were beginning to mover in on Fatboy's territory. He was not only putting the organization in danger but also the people who worked for it. Their rivals were no longer scared. Steps had to be taken to put matters back on an even keel.

When Jaimie woke up each morning, he would sniff a line of coke that he had already cut the night before from his dressing table. He could not operate without the drug. Fatboy did not seem to care. In fact, he encouraged it. Addicts like to have company; it endorses what they do.

Jaimie's fitness disappeared quickly. He became flabby, his skin grey and sweaty. He nursed dreams of revenge for Simon's death. The 'Ndrangheta were too much to take on as an organization but if he could identify the men that killed his friend then surely individual retribution was not impossible? His opportunity soon came. Fatboy realized that he could not run his operation without the support of the Italians. It was time to sue for peace. A meeting was set up.

Jaimie accompanied Fatboy to the meeting with the 'Ndrangheta. It was an old abandoned fire station. The business was conducted standing up. Arthur Junior handed over an envelope. It contained forty thousand pounds. "I am very sorry for the misunderstanding," he said. "I hope that we can continue to do business?"

The lead negotiator was called Aldo. He nodded. "At the new price, yes. And perhaps send somebody who doesn't help himself to the money, no?" The Italian smiled. "Your delivery boy was a thief. We did you a favour, so no hard feelings?"

"None at all. He was my father's man, not mine. I always hated him," said Fatboy. "Fucking Yid."

Jaimie felt bile surge in his throat. He swallowed and blinked back tears. After the meeting, as he drove away, he realised what had to be done. It had to be done alone. He couldn't risk taking an accomplice into his confidence. If things failed and it came out later that he was responsible Jaimie knew that Arthur would have him crucified.

Early one Sunday morning while it was still dark Jaimie left his flat carrying a holdall. In the bag was a can of petrol and a sawn-off shotgun with a handgun for backup. He had had his eye on an old Land Rover, which was always parked at night on the kerb two streets away. He knew that it would have no alarm; it was a perfect height and fucking easy to steal.

Jaimie parked 50 yards from the newsagent. He knew Fatboy always took his dog for a walk to the newsagents first thing on a Sunday morning before retiring to bed for the rest of the day. He sat and waited, the peak of a baseball cap pulled over his face.

He spotted his target in the distance, plodding along behind the straining leash of his spaniel. There was nobody else about. As he approached Jaimie wound the car window down. "Jamsie, my boy!" said Fatboy smiling then looking confused as he noticed the car. Jaimie pulled the sawn-off from his lap and fired. His victim sprawled backwards. He fired again but he knew that was unnecessary. He knew that Fatboy was dead.

Within an hour the car was on fire parked in dense woodland and the shotgun was in the Clyde.

Aldo Contarda flicked the key fob and the lights on his Ferrari Testarossa winked on and off. There was a dull thud as the doors unlocked. It had been a long evening. The Albanians were hard negotiators and even harder drinkers. He needed to sleep but at this time of night if he drove fast, he would be home and in his bed in half an hour.

Within fifteen minutes he was out of the city. The car swept down the country road to his house. It was after midnight so there would be no traffic and his car could easily handle the turns on the narrow lane. He did not notice the stinger flicked across the road from a lay-by, but he did notice that the steering went light and out of control. The Ferrari hit a bank and flipped over, spinning on its roof.

As the car came to a stop, Aldo was hanging upside down from his seatbelt. He reached for the door handle and pulled. It would not open. The electrics had gone. As he struggled, he saw a pair of feet and legs through the windscreen. He shouted to be rescued. Then he smelt gasoline. It was being poured from a container, it glugged out in a puddle around the upturned car. The feet and legs moved away, dribbling a small line of petrol from the container, and then disappeared from his view. Aldo heard a muted thud, almost like a door slamming shut, as the burning cigarette met the petrol. He saw a bright orange glow and screamed.

Jaimie didn't often feel remorse, but he did when he called on Arthur to pay his respects. He had never seen him cry before and his wife, Mary, was inconsolable. Within a week another stroke had finished Arthur off, almost certainly because of his only son's death. "I'll look after everything for you," Jaimie said to Mary when he called round to the house for the second time that week. There were two funerals to arrange and a business to run.

As Jaimie took control of his new organization he began to understand that he had new responsibilities. His role had changed. It was more about using your head and less about using your fists. In many ways he saw his new position as akin to that of his hero, Kenny Dalglish, who had swopped his playing boots for the manager's job at Liverpool Football Club. Jaimie was no longer in the dressing room with the lads; he was in the manager's office on his own. He had to show his Italian partners that there was a new sheriff in town. A sober and responsible one who could be trusted and relied on.

Slowly, Jaimie began to get back on side with the 'Ndrangheta. There was so little left of Aldo Contarda's Ferrari it had been impossible to determine exactly what had happened. The police assumed that it was an accident caused by a driver speeding on a narrow country road while drunk. Whilst, the Italians might not believe that, if Jaimie's gang had anything to do with it the men who ordered the hit, Arthur and Fatboy, were dead.

Jaimie dropped the drugs. He would do a line now and again but only if the social situation dictated that he should. He still drank but when Janine came into his life he even stopped doing this at home and restricted his bevvying to occasional nights out with the boys.

He had had lots of women. They came with the job. Mostly he met them in nightclubs where he was pissed and so were they. Attracted by the glamour of a gangster's lifestyle, usually they were after the money or the drugs, or both, and inevitably these relationships always fell apart as he came to distrust their motives, or they became a liability.

Janine was different. He met her when he went to get his hair cut at a smart salon on Buchanan Street. She was the stylist who was given the job of taming his mop of thick black hair. She asked him questions and smiled and laughed at his replies. They quickly found a rapport. The next time Jaimie made an appointment he made sure that Janine was booked to do it. This continued for four months before Jaimie was confident enough to ask her on a date.

Jaimie and Janine had married the following year. It was a typical gangster's wedding: beautiful suits, flash cars and Cristal champagne being sprayed around. Janine revelled in the day. She loved being surrounded by all their friends and family. She knew nothing of Jaimie's drug dealing and he was keen to keep it that way.

Janine was a beautiful girl who was innocent of the darker side of the human soul, a place that Jaimie had always inhabited. That was why he loved her, and he intended to keep his business dealings as far away from their lovely new life as possible.

"She doesn't really know what you do, does she?" whispered Paul, Janine's brother as they stood at the reception bar.

"No, and she had better not find out," said Jaimie staring into his new bother-in-law's eyes.

As Jaimie stood for a group picture after the ceremony he was aware that it was not only the wedding photographer taking the pictures, he was certain that somewhere nearby was a member of the Drugs Squad with a long-angled lens snapping away. Jaimie knew that he had new responsibilities and that he had to be careful.

Chapter 12

Jaimie stared at the copy of the Daily Record on his desk, shook his head and sighed. "Massive Drugs Seizure in Glasgow," the headline read.

"Drugs with a street value of £2 million have been seized by officers of Police Scotland's new Organised Crime and Counter Terrorism Unit," the article read. "On 3rd April, approximately 20 kilograms of drugs, believed to be heroin and cocaine, were recovered from an address in Tollcross Road, Glasgow. One man aged 28 was arrested in connection with the incident."

Tollcross Road was a scruffy lock up and the drugs had been hidden in specially engineered compartments in an old transit van parked inside. The man arrested was Billy Caldwell, one of Jaimie's boys who was now on remand in Barlinnie Prison.

Richard Brown, Jaimie's lawyer and Company Secretary at Thistle Steel was seated across the desk. He was a dapper man in his early sixties with a neat grey moustache and although originally from Edinburgh he sounded more like Prince Charles than Bonnie Prince Charlie.

Before Jaimie took over, he had worked for Arthur. Originally trained as a certified accountant he had then studied Law at Glasgow University. On graduating he specialised in Corporate Law, but this had widened to include Criminal Law once he got involved with Arthur. Getting his client off the British Steel corruption charges had burnished his reputation with the Glasgow underworld. "Of all the criminals I have met he's the biggest," Arthur used to say. Jaimie always thought that he was like Mr. Burns in the Simpsons cartoon.

"So, what happened?" asked Jaimie.

"Billy told me that the police knew exactly where to look. He was asleep in the back of the van ready to move the stuff on in the morning when they broke open the doors with sledgehammers in the early hours. They had stripped the van and found the whole stash within an hour. Billy thinks that they must have been tipped off. I think so too. It must be the Albanians," said Richard.

Jaimie sighed again. Things in the drugs business had got tougher. Because of the terrorist crackdown money had become harder to launder and the police had been given more powers to monitor any computer or telephone activity.

The price of drugs had fallen too due to competition from the Albanian gangs. They had first started appearing in Glasgow in the mid-1990s. Claiming to be Kosovan refugees they had sought asylum in the UK. The Albanian gangs were already very sophisticated when they arrived in Scotland. Like the Sicilian mafia the roots of the gangs stretched back hundreds of years and were based on extended family connections. They had operated the black market during the repressive and reclusive regime of Eric Hoxha and after his death they were the people who made things work in the crumbling Albanian state. They had links with the Turkish mafia and assisted them with the movement of heroin from the poppy fields of Asia to the streets of Europe.

When they arrived in the UK the Albanians discovered that there were far greater profits to be made trading in Britain's buoyant cocaine market and for the first time since Fat Boy died Jaimie had serious competition on his hands. As well as the Albanian gangs' capabilities for the smuggling of drugs, people and firearms through dodgy haulage firms and corrupt border officials they were also notoriously violent and scared of no one. Even a hard man of the calibre of Jaimie McGovern found their excesses stomach churning. Their violence usually involved torture and mutilation. They also offered the punters pure cocaine so the days of cutting a batch with laundry detergent or baking powder and making an extra profit were gone.

It seemed to Jaimie that in the drugs business the stakes grew higher and the returns grew less.

"Is Billy okay?" asked Jaimie.

"He's scared. It's not surprising really, he's looking at 16 years and he'll probably serve half of that. He's a sensible lad though and knows not to talk. Your boys in Barlinnie have got that message to him too. I've told him that he will be looked after. Don't worry, he won't do anything silly," said Richard.

Jaimie pondered for a moment, his head down staring at the floor. "I haven't paid for the stuff they seized yet, it only came in yesterday," he said darkly.

"Two million is a lot to find," said Richard.

"That's the street value," said Jaimie. "I actually owe the Mob about 1.2 million."

"Well, yes," said Richard "but in the meantime you have nothing to sell and will lose market share due to unreliability and there are no profits from this batch to be reinvested because it has all been seized. It's a cashflow problem if nothing else. Can you get the Italians to share some of the pain with you?"

"No. They will say it's my problem and they will be right. There's no getting around paying it though and that's going to hurt my operation. Bastard Albanians! It's not as if I can claim on the insurance is it?" he shouted.

"Actually, I might be able to help you there," smiled Richard who opened his briefcase and pulled out a letter which he pushed over the desk to Jaimie.

The letter was headed Surety and Guarantee PLC. "**Are Bad Debts a Problem for Your Business**?" the headline in a bold font read. Jaimie looked at the text:

30th June 2006

Dear Mr. Brown,

Every year British businesses experience thousands of bad debts. At best these are a nuisance and can affect the profitability of your business but if the debt is large enough it could cause the insolvency of your company.

Credit Insurance is a solution to this problem. It allows the creditworthiness of your customers to be checked by professional risk managers on an ongoing basis, but should the worst happen, and your client goes bust the policy pays out 90% of the debt.

To find out more please call our Glasgow office on 0141 239 4400.

Yours sincerely,

James McDonald

New Business Executive

Jaimie blinked and then looked again at the letter. "How does this help me?"

Richard nodded acknowledging his client's confusion. "This was sent to my office the other day and it got me thinking," he said. "It's an old idea but with the addition of Credit Insurance we can give it a modern twist. You remember that Arthur used to move in on businesses that were doing really well, take a partnership, get goods on credit he could easily sell and then go bust so all the suppliers were left holding the baby?"

Jaimie nodded, "Yes, the old Long Firm game."

"Exactly," Richard said. "I thought we could do the same. We need to look for a steel stockholder which is well established, creditworthy you know, but where the owner is looking to sell up and retire or to take a back seat in running the business."

"Why in steel stockholding?" asked Jaimie.

"Because Mr. McGovern Thistle Steel is going to become his main supplier, at least on paper. We need a man on the inside to be one of the main directors, one of our own associates to run the show but someone who can't be directly linked with you or Thistle Steel. We take out a policy with this outfit," he said waving the Surety and Guarantee letter at Jaimie.

Jaimie drummed his fingers on the desk and looked thoughtful.

Richard Brown continued: "We invoice for a delivery of a million quid's worth of steel that was never actually delivered, our associate puts the company receiving it into administration and we claim on the insurance. Easy. Plus, we sell off all the steel we get from other suppliers on credit. The insurance fraud plus the old Long Firm game should net us at least one and a half million and if this works, we can do it again.

"There are a few Credit Insurance companies to have a go at. The other advantage is that apart from paying the premium what we earn is straight profit. It's a lovely white-collar crime none of this wading through muck and bullets," he laughed.

Jaimie smiled and nodded his head faintly. Arthur was right, Richard was a crook. Christ, this is a bit different than fighting the Albanians for territory he thought. "I like it. How do we set it up?"

"It will take a while," Richard said. "Probably a few months. As ever the devil is in the detail and I need to find out exactly how these policies work. We also need to find a steel stockholder that we can move in on and decide which one of our boys will be the Trojan Horse. Leave it with me I'll get back to you. My cut is 25% by the way, okay with you?"

Jaimie nodded.

Chapter 13

Miles crunched on the corner of his toast.

"Hello daddy!" cried Evie as she clip-clopped into the kitchen dressed in her Cinderella outfit and a shiny pair of her mother's shoes. Kath smiled. Evie loved dressing up.

"Daddy is going to sleep in the woods tonight with some bears," said Miles leaning down from his kitchen stool to hug his daughter.

Evie looked shocked. "No, he isn't," said Kath. "Daddy will be sleeping in a tent and there won't be any bears," said Kath.

"Oh," said Evie looking disappointed.

Every year Surety and Guarantee arranged an "Away Day" for its senior managers. This year they were going to the Forest of Dean to be taught fieldcraft by ex-army personnel. This would involve learning how to make a fire, foraging for food and cooking it.

In public Miles would always ridicule such events saying that the only reason for them was to give the Personnel Director something to do. He saw though that taking people out of their everyday office environment could show his colleagues in a very different light.

He especially remembered going to a Paintballing day a few years ago. Kath had snorted derisively when he told her where he was going. The event had been held in a wood in Oxfordshire. His colleagues had been split into two opposing teams and been assigned a home base to defend. For one game a flag had been placed midway between the two home bases. The organizer explained that the purpose of the game was for one team to capture the flag and then take it to the opposing team's base without being shot on the way. A few minutes into the game Miles saw one of his teammates, Aidan, grab the flag and disappear behind a tree. The game continued for ten more minutes before the organizer blew the whistle to end the game.

"I blew the whistle because nothing was happening," he said. "Who's got the flag?"

All the contestants looked at each other each one either shrugging or shaking their heads. At that moment Aidan jogged into view carrying the flag. When asked where he had been he explained that he had run off to hide because if the other team didn't know where the flag was then they couldn't win. Some people are so scared of protecting what they have that they never take a risk. It was hard to think that Aidan had been the Sales Director. He was probably next in line to be the England football manager Miles mused.

Seven tents formed a circle in the forest clearing. In the centre was a large fire with a pan of frying rabbit and mushrooms on a trivet spitting away. Miles sat with the rest of his colleagues drinking beer and talking. The day had been sunny and dry, and the instructors had been friendly. Next to Miles sat an elderly man called Brian. Unlike the rest of the instructors he was not ex-military but was a professional forager and had shown the group how to identify plants and herbs that they could eat. The mushrooms frying over the fire were wild ceps that he had found.

"Have you always been a forager?" Miles asked.

"Yes, since I was a young boy," Miles nodded. "In those days I used to have this place to myself. My grandfather taught me how to catch fish, how to trap rabbits, squirrel and hedgehog."

"Hedgehog? What does that taste like?" asked Miles in amazement.

"It's a bit like chicken," Brian hesitated as he thought. "And a bit like cat." Miles laughed, and Brian looked at him blankly.

"I don't trap much now though," he added. "As you get older killing anything starts to be abhorrent to you. I used to find some of the animals in my traps still alive. It's the way they look at you," Brian shook his head and shuddered.

"I survive mainly on the plants, herbs and fungi. The odd fish. Before mankind became domesticated and started living on farms and in towns the forest would have provided for his every need: housing, heating, water, food and medicine. And pretty much the whole of this country would have been covered in forest.

"Ancient men were a lot stronger and healthier than us too. Civilization was a trap, which we fell into and have never been abler to get out of. The ancient peoples have gone. Aborigines, American Indians wiped out or brought to heel. The wisdom of a hundred thousand years discarded in few generations.

"I'm not a hippy," said Brian adjusting his ponytail, "but there's no variety anymore. Worldwide, people mainly eat four types of meat – beef, chicken, pork or lamb – and four types of grass- wheat, maize, rice and millet. People eat the same things all year round. You can buy strawberries in December." He shook his head and looked wistful. "Even when you watch the TV and see documentaries on tribes in the Amazon most of the kids are wearing Arsenal shirts," he sighed.

"But more people are starting to forage? Miles trying to offset the despondent turn in the conversation.

"Yes, but not many like me. Mainly they come during the mushroom season. Some pick wild mushrooms and sell them to restaurants. I wish they would bugger off. They don't just pick what they need but what they can make money from. It will destroy the eco-system if it is allowed to carry on. Others are only interested in picking magic mushrooms. There are many different types and they would have been well known to our ancestors. Most communities would have a shaman or medicine man who knew about the properties of each and this knowledge would have been passed down by word of mouth from generation to generation.

"Do you remember that they found a man who had been completely preserved in a glacier in the Italian Alps about 10 years ago?" Brian asked.

Miles nodded. He remembered reading about it in the newspapers and had a vague recollection of watching a TV documentary about it.

"They called him Otzi," Brian continued. "Two walkers found him. At first, they thought it was the body of a mountaineer who had died in a recent accident. When the authorities managed to extract the corpse from the ice, and it was taken to be examined properly, though they found it had been there for five thousand years.

"It was the best-preserved body they had ever found in Europe. He was fully clothed too. He had a cloak made of grasses, a jerkin, trousers, leather shoes and a bearskin cap. He also had a copper axe and arrows in a quiver. Most likely he was a hunter.

"There was a leather pouch on his belt. There were various tools in there and two types of mushroom. One of them was quite unusual; it's called a Birch polypore.

It grows on the side of Birch trees. Later, a CAT scan was done on the corpse and found out that poor old Otzi suffered from something called whipworm. It's an intestinal parasite. Now, what do you think the best medical treatment for whipworm was? Yes, Birch polypore! Now how on earth did he know that unless it was wisdom that had been passed down to him? He didn't have a laboratory to do medical testing. He probably didn't even know what was wrong with him and yet he was able to find the one thing in the forest that could cure him. Isn't that amazing?"

Brian paused for a few seconds and took a swig from his bottle of beer. He lived a solitary life and he loved having an audience. He could see that some of the other people who were huddled around the fire were listening to him too. Miles could understand why Outdoor Adventure employed the guy: his stories were fascinating.

"When Julius Caesar tried to invade Britain in 56 B.C. his army reported that the Ancient Britons they were fighting were completely unafraid to die," Brian continued. " The battles the Romans fought in Britain were so fierce that they completely gave up on the place and didn't come back for another hundred years. I think our guys had probably taken some type of psilocybin mushrooms, so they could feel no pain.

"Like morphine today the shamans would have used mushrooms to make the passing of people quicker and more tolerable too. A lot of people who pick have very little idea of what they are doing though. It can be very dangerous. I have heard of people taking Magic Mushrooms who have been paralysed for hours, completely unable to move. Others have violent hallucinations and end up in a terrible state."

"Is it easy to identify poisonous mushrooms?" Miles asked

"No. It's pretty difficult. Some of the most poisonous look very like the ones that you can eat. Like I said this afternoon although this is a bit of fun I would never advise people to pick and eat wild mushrooms unless they knew exactly what they were doing," Brian said.

"Eating just one Death Cap mushroom could kill you and they look like small Field Mushrooms. Apparently, they taste very good too, so there are no clues as to how toxic they are when you eat them. The end is nasty too, your get stomach cramps, vomiting, violent diarrhoea. Basically, your liver slowly packs up."

Miles cast a worried look at the frying pan. "Don't worry, I bought those from the supermarket, "Brian winked noticing his concern.

"Not a great way to commit suicide then?" laughed Miles.

"Oh God, no. The worst. The best way is digitalis," said Brian stroking his beard and gazing into the fire. "Foxgloves you know? Very clean. If you take the leaves and boil them up and then drink the liquid it would stop your heart dead in a few hours. If it's concentrated enough it will kill you pretty much instantaneously. Have you have had to put an animal down?"

Miles nodded. He thought about how he, Kath and Evie had sat and cried together after the vet had given a lethal injection to their cat, Sooty. He remembered the soft rattle in their beloved pet's throat. How he had become very still and how the light had left his eyes.

It can be that quick. And almost undetectable," Brian mused. "You boil it down into a clear liquid. It's tasteless and it doesn't smell of anything either. Unless a pathologist knew what he was looking for it looks like a heart attack."

Brian came out of his reverie and looked at Miles. "Christ, I shouldn't be telling you this. Don't you fellows do Life Insurance? I am giving away the tricks of the trade, how to top yourself and still get the policy to pay out. You'll be in the office on Monday morning telling your claims inspectors to check anybody who dies of a heart attack."

"Not my type of insurance, don't worry," Miles laughed.

"Oh good, my exit plan is still safe then," smiled Brian.

Chapter 14

Richard Brown had been busy. In the days following his meeting with Jaimie McGovern he had arranged a meeting with the local representative of Surety and Guarantee and had identified a steel stockholder in Lincolnshire that with some negotiation, and failing that some threats, could come under their control.

Richard Brown had spoken to James McDonald, the young man at Surety and Guarantee who had sent him the letter and arranged to meet him at the insurance company's local offices.

James McDonald was in his early 20s. He was dressed in a cheap suit, with pointy brown shoes and heavily gelled hair. He had the excitement and enthusiasm of a Labrador puppy. Richard loved these qualities in salesmen. James was too inexperienced to be hard bitten and cynical. All critical faculties, if he ever possessed any, had been suspended in pursuit of closing a deal. He could be milked for any information required and would never stop to wonder why.

Richard introduced himself as a solicitor acting on behalf of a client the name of which he could not disclose but who had expressed an interest in finding out more about credit insurance.

The young man nodded eagerly and launched into a series of questions about the business that was looking for cover. Very soon it was established that for the very modest price of around £20,000 an annual policy could be taken out.

"That seems reasonable, said Richard. James nodded eagerly. "Now, does that give full cover on all customers?"

"Well it can," said James, shuffling uncomfortably. "You see we vet the creditworthiness of your customers," answered James. "You apply for cover using our online link. You tell us which customer you need cover on and for how much."

"So, we make an application on, for example, ABC Ltd and say we need £20k cover a month, is that how it works?"

"Not quite," said James. "You apply for the maximum amount they are likely to owe you. So, if you offer a customer 60-day terms and they pay you a month late, which is quite typical, then they owe you for 90 days' worth of trading, or £60k using your example of £20k a month. It's what we call an insured limit."

Richard nodded. "And how do you arrive at an insured limit?" Richard asked. "Do your underwriters simply look at the accounts filed at Companies House?"

"We do use filed accounts, but that information can be somewhat historic." James acknowledged. "So, we also approach companies for information that is not in the public domain, like management accounts. We find out who their principal suppliers are and things like that. The rule of thumb is that provided a company is profitable then the credit limit is about 20% of the net worth, but it can go higher than this if there are other factors we can consider. The underwriter in charge of writing these limits is called Bill Thompson. He's a real expert in the steel business."

Richard made a note in his Black and Red notebook. "If we decide to go ahead, I should like to meet him," he smiled.

"Oh, that won't be a problem at all," said James flushing in excitement.

Archie Styles was 66. He had been in the steel industry for over 50 years and for the past 30 years had been the owner and Managing Director of Gainsborough Steel Traders Ltd. He had steered his business through economic ups and downs and the ever-changing price of steel but now he felt he couldn't go on. Betty, his wife, had Multiple Sclerosis. This had been diagnosed many years before but now she was confined to a wheelchair and sometimes unable to get out of bed for days. He knew that Betty probably didn't have long left and that he needed to spend more time with her as her health spiralled inevitably down.

Archie and Betty had two sons, but Michael lived in Canada and David had a good job in London. Neither was interested in returning to the wilds of Lincolnshire to help continue the family business. Quietly his business had been up for sale for the past two years, but nobody had expressed an interest in buying it. It was a small family business and had been deliberately run to avoid tax so the returns in the annual accounts were modest. Archie feared that one day he would have to simply close the doors and walk away.

Archie had bought intermittently from Thistle Steel, particularly in the early years of his business when their prices were significantly cheaper than anybody else's and they didn't seem to worry about the amount of credit they gave. These days he used them when he needed to source a particular type of steel in a hurry but he had always paid for what he bought on the nail.

He had heard that Thistle had a very shady reputation, particularly when Arthur had been in charge.

He received a telephone call one morning in February as he was sitting at his desk nursing a cup of coffee and staring out of his window into the bleak, grey yard which was piled high with steel coil. It was Jaimie McGovern. Archie knew Jaimie only very slightly having been introduced to him at the Annual Steel Stockholders Association Dinner, which was usually held at a swanky hotel on Park Lane. Intriguingly, Jaimie said that he wanted to meet to discuss a business proposition and suggested that he and a colleague drove down to Gainsborough the following week to take Archie out to dinner.

Initially Jaimie had not wanted to involve himself in the negotiations with Archie Styles. He had felt it best if he remained in the background, but Richard had persuaded him that the offer they were going to make would not look attractive without the reputation of Thistle Steel behind it.

Jaimie and Richard took Archie to dinner at a smart hotel in Gainsborough. For most of the meal they exchanged niceties about business and the steel trade. It was only as the after-dinner drinks were being served to them in the hotel's comfortable lounge that Richard cut to the chase.

"Thank you for agreeing to see us Archie," he smiled. "The reason we are here is that we are interested in making an offer for Gainsborough Steel Traders." Archie tried hard not to let his excitement show.

Richard went on to explain that Thistle Steel were looking for a distributor in the North of England and that Archie's company fitted the bill. "It won't be directly linked to Thistle Steel though. We don't want our competition to make a direct connection and there are other tax reasons," said Richard waving his hand airily.

Archie nodded pretending that he understood what the man was talking about. He was a simple man. His head spun every year when the auditors compiled his accounts. Half the time he had no idea what they were talking about and usually acted on the instructions of his accountant without ever questioning him.

"Gainsborough Steel will still continue to be an independent business, but Thistle Steel will become its main supplier. You can obviously see the benefits in such a link, you will be able to buy steel at a discount. It should increase your profitability dramatically."

Archie pondered for a moment. "You said that "I" will be able to buy steel at a discount. I won't be involved though. You want to buy the business off me don't you?"

"Well yes," said Richard unctuously. "But you have spent years building up this business, we wouldn't want to lose the goodwill and contacts you have overnight."

"But I want to retire, my wife's not well you see…" Archie's voiced trailed off. He looked as if he were about to cry.

"I know, I have heard. I'm so sorry," said Richard soothingly. "We do envisage you being able to put your feet up. To take a back seat. We want to put our own man in to run things day-to-day. All you must do is to maintain your contacts, your customer base, the odd lunch here and there. You don't even have to come into the office unless you want to."

Archie looked brighter. "So, who will be running it?"

"Jaimie's brother-in-law, Paul." Jaimie who had said nothing until now nodded his head and smiled. "He's a good lad. He has worked in Thistle for a few years now and know all the ropes. He can easily manage your operation and if things ever get a bit sticky he can always call me or Richard."

"But if I'm not selling the business how do I get paid?" said Archie looking puzzled.

"Well you will be selling us the business, but over a period of time" said Richard. "Now, I have looked at your accounts and I value the business at about half a million."

"Archie looked disappointed. "I was hoping for a bit more than that," he said.

"I understand, but the offer is a bit more generous than that," said Richard. "What we have in mind is that we agree a price and then we take a 51% shareholding, or at least Paul will, so that he has a controlling interest. We agree to pay you £125,000 out of the profits each year every year plus a dividend. You have easily made £200k profit in each of the last five years so there will be enough to cover that, plus we plan to expand the business, so your dividend payment should increase every year.

"Once the annual £125k is paid your shareholding reduces by 10%, it will transfer to Paul, until after four years you have a 9% shareholding. You can continue to keep the remaining shareholding as a sort of pension or chose to sell it. It should be a very good investment. Over this period, you continue to be a Director and an employee of the company and we pay you an annual salary. We were thinking £50,000."

Richard could afford to be generous. The deal presupposed that Gainsborough Steel Traders Ltd would continue to trade successfully. Once he had gained control he knew that in a few months it would be a burned-out shell. The company was simply a vehicle to perpetrate a fraud. A getaway car to be abandoned and set alight after a heist. The guy sitting in front of him would lose everything. Fucking idiot.

"What if I die in those five years or I am too ill to work?" asked Archie.

"Well you would still have the security of your shareholding. It can be willed to any beneficiary. We would still have to buy it," Richard said reassuringly.

Archie lowered his head, trying to disguise a smile. "Let me have a think about it over the weekend," he said. "I will let you have my answer on Monday."

"Absolutely, take your time," said Richard. The man had his head in the trap and was just about to take the bait.

Chapter 15

Richard Brown leaned his head around Jaimie McGovern's office door. "We are all ready to go," he said. "The guys from Surety and Guarantee are coming in at eleven."

"Excellent," said Jaimie and smirked as a mental image of Mr. Burns came into his head.

In the previous ten weeks things had moved on quickly. Following their meeting, Archie Styles had 'phoned to say that he would like to take up the offer. Richard had drawn up the papers for signing. Archie had used a local solicitor to look over the agreement. Somebody who was used to house sales rather than business sales. Cheap and useless, Richard thought. Following a swift conclusion, Paul Jones, Jaimie's brother-in-law had been installed as the new Managing Director and majority shareholder.

Richard had got to work quickly. He had heeded the advice that Surety and Guarantee would usually set a credit limit on a company of 20% of the net worth. Based on the last filed accounts Gainsborough Steel had a net worth of only £600k, so he could only reasonably expect to get an insured limit of £120k, which was miles away from the £1 million he needed to make the fraud worthwhile.

He had brought all his accounting whiles to this problem. First, he started to revalue all the assets. This mainly included the value of the yard and its buildings, three trucks and the stock in the yard. Richard realised that the yard had last been valued ten years ago for the modest sum of £300k. Commercial property values had not increased hugely in that time, but Richard thought that realistically he could get it revalued at £500k. By using a friendly valuer, that is to say a crooked one, he had managed to get it revalued at £750k.

Richard also used a friendly auditor to prepare Gainsborough Steel's annual accounts. He brought in £500k of steel from Thistle to sit in the yard for a few days before it was sent back to increase the stock value from £200k to £700k. The trucks were revalued too, and, in the end, he had managed to push the asset value up to £1.5 million.

Richard had sweated the assets as much as he could, but he would still probably only be able to get an insured limit of £300k on Gainsborough. He was still massively short of his target. Jaimie wasn't going to be pleased with him if all this effort had been for nothing. Reluctantly he decided that Gainsborough Steel needed a significant cash injection.

"You can put it in and take it out the day after the accounts are finalised," he told Jaimie, who had grumbled and shook his head. Eventually, it was agreed that £500k would be very temporarily lent by Thistle to Gainsborough Steel.

With the existing cash balance of £73k, that gave a total asset value of £2,073,000. That would still only give an insured limit of just over £400k. Richard knew he would have to be on his mettle for his forthcoming meeting with Surety and Guarantee. He thought that James McDonald would be malleable enough, but would Bill Thompson, the senior risk underwriter who was coming from head office? Richard had done his homework though and thought that he stood a reasonable chance.

James McDonald sat in the short stay car park of Glasgow Central railway station. He watched as Bill Thompson lurched towards the car a polystyrene cup of coffee in one hand, a copy of The Racing Post under his arm and a Marlboro jammed between the yellow fingers of his other hand. He flicked his cigarette into the gutter before opening the passenger door.

"Hello Bill," simpered James.

"Wanker," said Tom with a brief nod. James laughed but with no warmth. Arrogant bastard he thought.

It was true that Bill Thompson was arrogant, but it had not always been so. The steel industry was inhabited by men who in other times might have sailed under the Jolly Roger or had gunfights at the O.K. Corral. In such company it was important to make one's mark, but it certainly wasn't the person his mother would have recognised.

When he returned to the family home, a plush country estate in Norfolk, at Christmas – and that was the only time he went home – he had a rather plummy accent and referred to his parents as "Mummy" and "Daddy." His bluster and heavy drinking were to hide a desperate shyness formed from being sent away as a boarder to a minor Public school in Rutland at the age of eight.

Noting that most of the people he encountered spoke in regional accents he had slowly changed his voice from the received pronunciation of the Public School to the Estuary English of most of his work contemporaries. It had started off as Mick Jagger, but years of drinking and smoking had left it more like that of his hero Keith Richards, a man who Bill Thompson set all his standards by.

As a young underwriter he had been taken to the infamous Soho drinking den, the Colony Room Club. At first, he was shocked that the fierce barmaid, Muriel, seemed to refer to all the members as "Cunty." She had picked on him on his first visit. "Hey cunty, buy another drink or fuck off back to the children's home."

He had become a regular because the place was open way into the early hours, and he saw how much the clientele liked being abused by her. She was like Basil Fawlty with Tourette's. Quickly he followed suit and started referring to anybody who was younger than him or who he considered to be inferior as "Wanker." If you started off by intimidating people, they always seemed to like you better when you were nice to them he had always found.

James parked in one of the empty spaces outside of Thistle Steel's offices. He and Bill walked into the building, reported at the desk and were issued with visitor's badges by the pretty receptionist. Richard Brown came down the stairs and shook their hands warmly before inviting them to follow him into the Boardroom.

James introduced Bill who then talked for about fifteen minutes about the steel industry and the people he knew. Coffee was brought by the receptionist and James began to discuss the quote. "I hope you don't mind James, but this is really only going to work for us if we can get the insured cover we require on our customers," said Richard cutting to the chase. "Now you have sent me a list of insured limits and you are a bit short on a few."

Richard started talking about a few accounts that he had no concern about getting the cover on. Bill either agreed them or asked for further information to be sent. "Now this is the most important one, Gainsborough Steel Stockholders," said Richard. "You have agreed a limit of £450k but this doesn't work for us. We really need a million. Bill produced a copy of the accounts from his briefcase, which was open on the desk. He felt that he had been generous on this, but the business had been trading for over 30 years with no problems and it had recently had a large capital injection. It looked like it could be worth backing.

"It is a bit difficult to justify more on this," he said. "Have you traded with them for long?"

"Yes, years," Richard lied. "In fact, we are their major supplier. I'd say 90% of the steel they supply comes from Thistle."

"That could make a difference," Bill nodded. "Can you send me some trading experience?"

"Give me a minute," said Richard and left the Boardroom. James McDonald had prepared him for this eventuality. On his desk was a print out of five years of trading experience with Gainsborough Steel. It was entirely fabricated but Richard knew that there was no way of checking this unless Bill 'phoned the customer to check, in which case he would simply end up talking to Paul who would verify everything.

Richard waited a few minutes before going back into the meeting. He used the time to reprint the trading experience he was going to give to Bill as he realised that the document's pages had to be warm so that it seemed that he was not prepared for this request. He entered the room and handed the papers to the underwriter.

After a few minutes' perusal, Bill lifted his head from the figures. "I could do £650k."

Richard looked concerned. This was not working out as anticipated. "I really need more."

Bill glanced at his watch. It was 12.47pm. The meeting had gone on too long already and he wanted a drink and a cigarette. He thought for a moment and looked at James. "Have you told him about top up cover?" he said. James looked confused and shook his head.

Bill rolled his eyes and tutted. He turned to look at Richard. "Top up cover is fairly new. If we get to the maximum insured limit that we can offer, in this case £650k, we can offer an additional product, which effectively doubles that cover. There is an extra cost, however. There is an annual charge of 2% of the value of the extra limit. Now you want a million of cover, so you only need £350k extra so the additional cost is £7k."

"But I could take the whole of the extra £650k if I wanted to?" said Richard. "So, I could have an insured limit of £1.3 million?"

"Well yes, but it would cost you an extra £13k," said Bill.

"That's a bit much, but I would like the full £1.3 million. We are planning to increase our business substantially with Gainsborough next year," said Richard, thinking that he should be nominated for next year's Oscars.

Bill took out his calculator and tapped for a few seconds. The information he was putting in meant bugger all. He knew what he was going to ask for, but he needed to make it look like it had been arrived at scientifically. "We could do it for 30 grand, how does that sound?"

Richard pretended to think. "How about £27k?" he said.

"28k and it's a deal," said Bill. James smiled.

"You have a deal then," Richard smiled back. "Let's get the paperwork done and I will take you out to lunch if you have time?"

"Ta. Do mind if I go outside for a fag while Chuckles finishes off here?" Bill said nodding towards James.

Richard smiled indulgently at Bill. This wasn't business. It was one man demonstrating to another how high he could piss up a wall. You can break all the rules and one day the rules will break you he thought.

James and Bill got back in the car. James had drunk only mineral water over lunch while Bill had started with a double gin and tonic, then drunk most of a bottle of Malbec which he had shared disproportionately with Richard Brown. He finished with a large cognac. "Come on wanker, my train is in half an hour and I want to get a six pack before I get on otherwise I've got five hours with fuck all to do," said Bill.

"It should only take ten minutes," said James who was happy that the deal was closed but had grown very tired of his colleague's condescending manner. He looked at Bill as he turned the key in the ignition. "I thought we were only allowed to sell top up cover to clients who had been with us at least five years and had a good claim's history?" he said.

"That's just to stop you arseholes going mad and selling it to any shit piece of business that rolls in," said Bill. "It'll be fine. I'll sort it." He paused to rub at a grease spot on his shirt. "No thanks required by the way," he said shaking his head in disgust at James when there was no response from his colleague. " Now, can we go wanker?"

Chapter 16

Richard had decided to bide his time before executing the fraud. Despite pressure from Jaimie he thought submitting a large claim within weeks of starting the policy with Surety and Guarantee would be sure to ring alarm bells. He was the ice to Jaimie's fire. It was a partnership that worked well for both. The Lennon and McCartney of the underworld.

As it turned out Gainsborough Steel was a good business. Yes, he had to pay Archie Styles over four grand a month, but this was easily covered. Provided the business was bust before Archie's first annual pay-off everything would be fine. Gainsborough were also a good little customer for Thistle, and he knew that a history of recent payments would make the whole thing look legitimate when the claims inspector at Surety and Guarantee came to pass his eye over it.

Richard Brown had gleaned all this information from James McDonald. He had discovered over the lunch with the drunken oaf, Bill Thompson, that James was a Rangers fan. A few invitations for the young man to Thistle's box at Ibrox had allowed Richard to pump James for information as to how the whole claims process worked in practice.

After the policy had been live for eight months Richard was ready to put his plan into action. He had continued to source steel from Gainsborough's traditional suppliers and had got Archie to order the goods so that most of them were unaware of the change in the company's status.

Richard issued several invoices from Thistle to Gainsborough over the next few weeks totalling just over £1.4 million. No steel was delivered but Paul Jones was given Delivery Notes to sign to say that he had received the goods. In the same way he had got Paul to drain his company's bank account.

Finally, Richard recalled the £500k loan that Thistle had made to Gainsborough so that it had no money left to pay suppliers. All the steel belonging to other supplies was put on trucks and shipped to Thistle's yard in Glasgow. A few weeks later Thistle issued a winding up order for unpaid goods. The company was bust, and a Receiver was appointed.

Richard had hoped that Thistle could appoint Gainsborough's Receiver. Thistle were entitled to do this as they were the largest creditor. He had a docile insolvency practitioner lined up, but Surety and Guarantee had insisted on taking the proxy vote at the Creditor's Meeting and appointed their own man. It was something that he had not considered. Still, the Receiver was there to collect outstanding debts and sell the assets not to look at the absence of any steel in the yard or ask questions about the withdrawn loan.

He could not manipulate matters in the way he wanted but Richard felt that he was on safe ground. The insurance claim would pay £1.3 million, plus there was the money that had been siphoned out of Gainsborough's cash reserves and perhaps another £400k of steel from other suppliers.

An unexpected bonus was that Richard realised that he could reclaim the Value Added Tax back on the bad debt too. This was even though no VAT relating to the Thistle debt had ever been handed over to HMRC. Like everybody else the Inland Revenue were a creditor of

Gainsborough Steel because there had simply been no money left when the company went bust. Not a cent. At the current rate of 17.5% that amounted to another £227,500. Not bad, for a transaction that merely existed on paper, with the added pleasure of taking the money off HMRC too.

He had a small concern that the Inland Revenue might further investigate this, but the payment of the Credit Insurance claim would give credence to the fact that the deliveries of steel existed even though they didn't. It was very neat. One hand washes the other, he thought. What is more is that any investigation would not get far if there were no directors of Gainsborough Steel to interrogate. Already, Paul Jones had been despatched on a long sojourn in the Far East.

Archie Styles was due to be despatched too. Richard Brown did not always approve of Jaimie's methods. Intimidation was one thing, but murder was quite another. Unfortunately, Archie Styles had been stupid. Reports of his bleating about being cheated by Jaimie and Richard had come to them from several sources. Left unchecked it was only a matter of time before somebody took these complaints seriously.

Richard was very careful never to be implicated in delivering these execution verdicts though. If matters came to a head a few years in an open prison for fraud would be tolerable, twenty-five years in some Victorian hellhole would be quite another matter.

£2,127,500 was a good return on an investment that had cost less than £150k, Richard mused. The trial run had been successful. There were half a dozen companies in London that offered Credit Insurance, and this would be a blueprint. He could easily make £10 million out of them he thought.

He realised that he couldn't always use Thistle as the vehicle for this but with his knowledge of Company Law and Accounting it would be easy enough to set up companies to perpetrate these frauds through. Why stop at the UK? There was Ireland. The USA perhaps? Europe? Languages would be a problem but that wasn't insurmountable. Then there was the whole field of invoice finance. I could get some of the money back that the bastards at the banks are happy to rip off from us, he thought.

Richard hated banks. The ringtone on his new mobile phone, something called an iPhone, was Bank Robber by the Clash, which made Jaimie laugh every time it rang.

The banks, the insurance companies, the utilities they were all criminals. All of them had their greedy snouts in the trough. What was the difference between giving a free wrap of heroin to a kid on the street to offering a teaser rate so that some school cleaner could buy a second home in Spain? Something that she couldn't possibly afford when the payments jumped up two years later. Not much he thought.

Richard continued to muse. It will all topple over one day and when it does, we will all be putting the blame on each other, he thought. And yet we are all culpable. All greedy bastards that won't be happy with what we have. At least those taking out the loans are probably just stupid though. The guys at the top perpetrating these scams will get away scot-free. Clever bastards. They will walk away with their millions into the sunset and the rest of us will have to pick up the bill. This wasn't a fraud; it was just a small act of revenge. They won't even miss it, he thought.

Still, it was more lucrative and a lot safer than the messy world of drugs.

Richard had attended an accountancy conference a few years ago at a smart hotel in Cheshire. One of the guest speakers was from the Fraud Squad. "The police simply do not have the resources to tackle fraud," he said. "Most of the people who work on scams are civilians, not policemen and if they were any good they would be working for the fraudsters, not us because the money is rubbish. If you are going to commit fraud unless it is high profile, I estimate your chances of getting away with it are 99%," he concluded.

Richard thought that he was an idiot for saying that. He might have well put a sandwich board outside every police station in the country saying: "Criminals Wanted, Accountancy Experience Preferable." Richard smiled at his own joke. He thought of a line from the song about the outlaw, Pretty Boy Floyd, by Woody Guthrie: "Some will rob you with a six-gun, And some with a fountain pen." He liked that.

Jaimie's secretary put her head around Richard's door. "Archie Styles is on the 'phone for you."

"Tell him I'm not in," said Richard.

Chapter 17

Miles looked at the Claim Form on his desk. It was for £1.3 million. Jesus! The client, Thistle Steel, had only been with them for just over 9 months. He looked through the supporting documentation. The debt had been confirmed by the Receiver. The invoices and delivery notes were in order. There's no getting out of this one, he thought as he put the form back in his In-Tray. The claim was over £1 million so he would have to do a full written assessment and then send it up to his Financial Director, Giles Smith, for sign-off.

He would attend to it later. Miles looked at his watch. It was 12.30 and as it was Friday he thought that he would walk to the pub, The Sea Lion, around the corner and catch up with his colleagues. When he entered the bar, he saw Bill Thompson perched on his normal stool at the bar. Miles usually only went to the pub at lunchtime on Friday, but Bill was there every day, at lunchtime and after work. "Hello, Bill," he said.

"Wanker," said Bill raising his glass in salute.

"That's the pot calling the kettle black mate," said Miles. "When was the last time you went out with someone?"

"You know me, young, free and single," said Bill.

"Well two out of three anyway," grinned Miles

Bill grinned back but there was no rejoinder. He never came off very well in these verbal battles with Miles and he realised it was time to shut up.

"Fucking hell, you look terrible," said Miles studying his colleague more closely.

"Hair of the dog mate," said Bill taking a long swig from his pint of Stella Artois. "I went to a Steel Stockholders golf day in Leeds yesterday. I've just got back."

"Did you play?" Miles asked.

Bill swayed his head from side to side "A bit, you know."

Bill was crap at all sports and had the fitness of a 94-year old. He had played the first three holes with some clubs that he had rented. His shot off the first tee hadn't gone more than five feet. "It didn't even reach the Ladies' tee, get your dick out," one of his playing partners had jeered while the others laughed.

After hacking round the next two holes, where he scored an eight and then a ten, Bill stood on the fourth tee and completely missed his shot, stumbling and only just able to stop himself from falling over. "It's no wonder you are playing so badly," one of his companions said, "you've got a big piece of shit on the end of your club." Bill turned the club upside down and looked at the head. There was nothing on it. "Other end," said his playing partner causing the other two to laugh raucously.

Feigning a twisted ankle from his stumble Bill had picked up his ball and headed for the nineteenth hole.

He sat nestled in a corner of the Clubhouse for the next two hours, hidden behind a trophy cabinet reading the newspaper and drinking lager. Eventually, the players started to trickle in. Bill didn't recognise anyone he knew so he remained in his seat trying to fill in The Times crossword and failing.

On the other side of the trophy cabinet he heard some of the returning players take a seat. They started their conversation talking about the round they had played, each one ignoring the other until it was their turn to talk. When they had finished their serial monologues, it went quiet for a few moments. "Did you hear about Archie Styles?"

"The lad from Gainsborough Steel?" another asked.

"Yes. He's dead. I went to his funeral last week. He threw himself in front of a train." Bill stopped looking at the crossword and started to listen more intently as the men tutted and clucked. "I spoke to his son after the service. His business went bust a few weeks ago. He said that his father was beside himself. He couldn't stop crying. He said that Thistle Steel had moved in on him last year and they had cheated him."

"That's Jaimie McGovern's outfit," a Scottish voice said. "Oh dear, he should have known better."

Bill had thought about the conversation on the train back to London that morning. He needed to know if Archie Style's demise had anything to do with the Credit Insurance policy he had sold to Thistle Steel. Given the conversation with Richard Brown about Gainsborough Steel he suspected that it might. He knew that he would have to approach this delicately. Selling top up cover to a new customer was almost certainly a sacking offence.

Bill relayed this information to Miles as they sat at the bar of the Sea Lion. He felt sick when Miles said he had a claim on his desk for £1.3 million. It would be better for Bill if the whole thing was rejected and then nobody would come to ask how the insured limit had been written in the first place. "It looks like a fraud to me," he said to Miles. "You need to investigate it some more before you send it up to the Giles for sign off." Miles nodded.

Miles started his investigation that afternoon when he returned to his office. First, he took company reports from the Companies House website on Thistle Steel Ltd and Gainsborough Steel Stockholders Ltd.

He watched as the printer spat out the information on A4 sheets of paper. It had not been that easy when he had started at Security and Guarantee. In those days if you needed the Report and Accounts on a company, they had to be obtained manually. One of his first jobs was to take a list of companies that his employer needed information on to the Companies House office on the City Road. He had to pay ten pence per report and sit and copy out the information onto a pad before taking it back to the underwriters at Surety and Guarantee. Miles had done that for six months and he remembered it as the most boring role he ever had. He supposed it must have always been this way since the company was founded in 1918. Even after that, company information was obtained by poring over microfiche records that made your eyes hurt.

Clients applied for credit limits by filling in forms and posting them! The replies would be returned in the same way. Looking back, it was almost Dickensian. Then came the telex machine, which made life easier.

Miles smiled as he remembered a story about when fax machines were first introduced. On the first morning they were installed one of the directors had asked Kath to fax a document to a client. He shouted at Kath when she returned the original document to him. "I told you to send it!" he had shouted at her, as if it was some sort of tele-transportation device. Miles and Kath had laughed about how clueless the directors were about new technology.

The company had been a lot different when Miles and Kath had started. There were banks of typists clacking away on ancient machines, using carbon paper to make copies and correcting mistakes with Tippex. Shorthand and Typing had been an exam option at school. Interestingly, it had only been offered as a CSE course though, as if it was too lowly a skill to merit an O Level.

All that had gone. First it was word processors, then typists had been done away with and everybody had their own PCs. Then the internet had rolled out. Miles remembered the first mobile phone. It was the size of a brick and had to be carried around in your briefcase. The phone was for the whole office to share and had to be specially booked out by those underwriters who were travelling to visit clients. The battery had to be charged all day and seemed to run out after half an hour's use. Most people seemed to use it only to call the office on their way home and say, "Hello, I'm on the train." Apple had just introduced a new smart phone. Miles didn't have one yet but had read that it could function as a phone and a computer that linked to the internet.

It was hard to think how the company had functioned before. It didn't seem to make people happier though, just more stressed and more demanding. These days people would apply for an insured limit on-line and then ring up five minutes later if the decision had not been agreed instantaneously. The technology boom had promised easier jobs with shorter hours. Instead, it had delivered a Sisyphean scenario: even when you were at home or on holiday there were still emails and telephone calls to answer.

He looked at the Thistle Steel report first. The Managing Director and principle shareholders were

Jaimie Ewan McGovern and his wife Janine. He looked again. He had heard that name before he thought but maybe the two pints of Guinness he had drunk in the pub were making him confused.

Financially Thistle Steel looked fine. The business was long established going back to the early 1960s and it looked to be a big player in the market. It certainly did not look like a vehicle that had been recently established just to perpetuate a fraud.

The trail ended there because he noted that the parent company was privately registered in Panama. Was there something to hide perhaps? Still, you could say the same about them he thought as he looked at the Starbucks logo on the takeaway coffee he had bought.

He turned his attention to Gainsborough Steel. This looked more suspicious. The principle shareholder had changed from Archibald Edwin Styles in the penultimate set of accounts to Paul Stephen Jones in the last set filed. The net worth had grown massively too. It had gone from being a tortoise to a hare. He noticed a substantial loan of £500k had been made. He needed to investigate that.

He picked up the 'phone and called his mate, Ron Jenkins. He had been at school with him and Ron had been the biggest thief that you were ever likely to meet. He had made the Artful Dodger look like Mother Teresa.

When they went into a café after going swimming when they were kids Ron would nick all the plates and cutlery. He had an early morning newspaper round across the Rye in East Dulwich. The guy who owned the newsagents loved Ron as he was always standing outside when the newsagents opened at 6am. Little did he know that Ron was helping himself to cartons of fags and Ronson lighters when the geezer went upstairs for his morning shit. He would sell this bounty at school in the playground. He would even take orders. "So that's a Mayfair, a Penthouse and two hundred Bensons. That'll be a fiver."

He had even stolen a three-wheeled light blue disabled car once so that he could sit down the front at Millwall. When "Only Fools and Horses" began on the television it was rumoured that it took Ron three episodes before he realised that it wasn't a fly-on-the-wall documentary.

It's funny how the biggest villains end up joining the police, Miles thought.

Miles was in luck. Ron was at his desk in Stratford nick. After chatting about old times for a few minutes Miles asked Ron to run the name Jaimie Ewan McGovern through the police computer. He heard a computer keyboard being tapped and then a low whistle. "Bloody hell mate, this one's a bad 'un. You should see this rap sheet. Drugs, violence, borstal, prison, the lot. There's a picture here too. It looks like it was taken at his wedding."

"Can you let me have a copy?" Miles asked.

"I'll print it off and meet you somewhere. Are you going to the game tomorrow?" Miles said he was. Millwall were playing Leeds at the New Den. "I'll see you in the Spotted Dog about one, how's that?" Miles agreed, and Ron was just about to end the call. "Can you look up one more name for me?" Ron sighed, "This ain't a public library you know? I'm not supposed to do this."

"Go on and I won't tell the Chief Constable about your paper round." Ron laughed. "This one is called Paul Stephen Jones."

"Make it easy for me why don't ya? You might as well just say John Smith."

"I only need to know if he is in any way associated with McGovern."

Ron looked at the computer screen. "Well McGovern's missus's maiden name was Smith," he said. "Listen, leave it with me and I'll see you tomorrow. We all fackin' hate Leeds." The line went dead.

The next day Miles stepped out of the entrance to Barking Tube Station turned left and headed for the Spotted Dog pub. Ron was standing at the bar as he entered. "Oi, oi," laughed Ron and pretended to jab him in the ribs. They ordered a couple of pints and found a table in the corner. After a few minutes chat about the fortunes of Millwall Ron pulled a brown A4 envelope out of the front of his Harrington jacket.

"Here, I'll be fucking glad to get rid of that, it's been sticking in my ribs all the way from Hornchurch," he said handing it over.

Miles pulled out a colour photograph. It was grainy because it had obviously been blown up. He studied it closely. He knew the guy's face. Then he realised how. It was the guy in the Glasgow hotel bar. How long ago was it? Four years? Five maybe. "That's him. That's McGovern. A real nasty piece of work by the looks of it," said Ron.

"How did you get on with Paul Jones?" he asked.

"Brother-in-law," said Ron taking a pull at his pint. "No form. Just an associate. Worked for Thistle Steel and then became the main director and shareholder in an outfit called Gainsborough Steel Stockholders. That outfit went bump, and it seems he has disappeared off on his travels. I have done some checking and it looks like he has been in Thailand for the past few weeks."

"That's really useful Ron, thanks," said Miles.

"No problem boy. Is that pie and mash place still open?"

Miles nodded. "Off we go then," said Ron draining his pint.

Chapter 18

On Monday morning Miles made a telephone call to the Receiver at Gainsborough Steel. Quite often insolvency practitioners were difficult people to deal with. A lot of what they did if not illegal was morally ambiguous. Surety and Guarantee gave a lot of work to this firm of accountants, however, and this usually secured some degree of cooperation from them.

Miles briefly explained to the Receiver who he was and that he was investigating a claim he had received as the result of the failure of Gainsborough Steel.

"How does it look to you?" he asked.

"Well the books are all in order," replied the Receiver, "but a lot of this doesn't fit together very well. There is almost no stock in the yard and yet a lot of creditors were owed money. It doesn't add up. I can't ask the Directors about it either because one has done a moonlight flit and the other has killed himself."

"There's no chance of any recoveries then?" Miles probed.

"No. We are going to have to liquidate the whole lot. In the accounts the yard is valued at £700k. Christ knows where they came up with that. I will be lucky if I can sell it for £200k. The trucks are knackered. There's no stock. I don't think the creditors are going to get anything back." Not after you have deducted your fees, Miles thought. Insolvency practitioners were appointed to act for the creditors but in his experience, they usually ended up acting for themselves.

"Anyway, why do you ask?" said the Receiver.

"I have had a big claim in from Thistle Steel. Before I pay it, I need to know that it is kosher. Do you think there may be an element of fraud involved here?" Miles asked.

"Maybe, but you need to be very careful if it concerns Thistle Steel. I was handling an Administration a few years ago and they turned up with three trucks saying they wanted to enforce their Retention of Title and take back any steel they had supplied that hadn't been paid for. Well, they took everything in the yard. It was probably ninety grand's worth of stock and they were owed less than ten. I wasn't going to stop them though.

"One of my colleagues had tried to do that with them before. He was handling another insolvency and they turned up mob handed again. He refused to let them take any stock until he had looked at the paperwork. Anyway, while he was upstairs in the office they crushed his Jag, which was parked in the yard, by pushing it into a wall with one of their trucks. When he complained they said it was an accident and that he should claim on his insurance. He could have called the police I suppose but discretion is the better part of valour when you are dealing with people like that.

"My advice is to be very careful how you tread with this. These guys don't play by our rules."

"One last thing, you said the books were in order so can you check something for me please?" Miles asked.
" In March last year there was a loan made to Gainsborough of £500k. It was subsequently called in which caused the business to collapse. Have you any idea who made that loan?"

"Let me check and I will come back to you," said the Receiver. Miles gave him his mobile number. An hour later he called back. "The loan was made by Thistle Steel," he said.

Miles sat at his desk and stared out of the window, he could see the traffic and the people in the street below. This was a fraud. He was certain of it. There were links by family and financially. There was collusion. The rigged accounts, the absence of stock and the main shareholder disappearing off to Thailand plus the story Bill Thompson had told him about the suicide of Archie Styles all pointed to only one conclusion.

In normal circumstances he would simply write to the company and reject the claim and if they wanted to take Surety and Guarantee to court then let them. But Thistle Steel was run by a gangster with a criminal background. As well as anecdotal evidence he had direct experience of the violence Jaimie McGovern and his thugs were prepared to resort to.

"Be very careful how you tread with this," said the Receiver. "Discretion is the better part of valour." He was right. But how can I pay out a claim when Bill Thompson has told me it was a fraud? He's a drunk and if he's told me then he's told everybody else in this building.

The claim was £1.3 million too. The amount was above his authorisation. Could he get away with paying a lower amount? Perhaps up to the maximum £1 million he was allowed to sign off? Maybe he should just come clean and report his suspicions to the Financial Director? But if he did that then the claim was certain to be turned down and it would still be his name was on the letter to Jaimie McGovern. What were Surety and Guarantee going to do? Put an armed guard around him and Kath and Evie?

In the end, the problem still came back to him. He would do whatever was necessary to protect his wife and his little girl. He put his mobile in his briefcase and closed it. "I'm going home, I don't feel very well," he told Rob Hatton who sat next to him. "I have let Personnel know." He really wasn't feeling good. The dilemma gnawed at brain. He needed a drink and he stopped off at a pub outside Liverpool Street station to satisfy that urge.

Chapter 19

Miles wrestled with the problem of the Thistle Steel claim for a few days. Kath had noticed that he was irritable and was drinking far more than he usually did. In fact, Miles never drank during the week, so she was surprised to notice that the glass-recycling bin was nearly full of empty bottles of red wine when she dragged it out on to the grass verge in front of their house for collection the next morning.

He was not sleeping either. He was normally a man who was asleep within a minute of turning out the bedroom light. Now he was restless, constantly altering his position. One night she woke to find her husband staring at the ceiling.

"What's wrong love?" she asked reaching for his hand. Miles shook it away. "It's just work. Go back to sleep."

She sat up and switched the light on. "Can I help? Is it something you want to talk about?"

"No. It's just a problem I need to think through," Miles said. He gave her a little smile and tapped her fingers with his own. "Don't worry. I can sort it out."

Over the following weekend Miles came to a decision. He was over thinking the problem, he realized and seeing threats that probably did not even exist. Jaimie McGovern was a drugs baron, He probably had very little to do with Thistle Steel and, besides, surely £1.3 million was a drop in the ocean to people like him?

Anyway, Thistle Steel was in Glasgow and Miles worked in London. Was there really any physical danger when the one location was so remote from the other? No, Miles decided.

The proper course of action would be to reject the claim. He would not accuse anybody of fraud but simply write to Thistle Steel in the morning saying that he was rejecting the claim due to "disparities." They could make from that what they will but would probably realize that their scheme had been rumbled and move on to something else. Miles's dad, Harry, had always said "face your problems, son." That is what he would do.

Over two weeks had elapsed since Miles had written to Thistle Steel rejecting their claim. He was beginning to think his approach had worked. It had been the correct call. He had faced the problem down. The telephone on his desk rang. Miles picked it up. "There's a gentleman here to see you Miles," said the receptionist.

Miles had not been expecting to see anybody that morning. "Who is it?" he asked.

"It's a gentleman called Richard Brown, from Thistle Steel."

Miles went silent. "Do you want to come down or shall I bring him up?" asked the receptionist.

Miles exited the lift and walked into the reception area of Surety and Guarantee. Standing in the middle of the room was an elderly man. He wore a black suit and shoes with a dark Crombie overcoat. He was holding the handle of his briefcase with both hands, his weight spread evenly. He stared menacingly at Miles as he approached, his face set in an impassive grimace.

"Mr. Brown?" said Miles.

"Please to meet you?" said Richard Brown who smiled thinly, who put his briefcase on the floor and extended his hand. "I have come to discuss a letter you sent to me recently rejecting a claim on Gainsborough Steel."

Miles took the man's hand. He looked flustered. "I wasn't expecting your visit, Mr. Brown. I am rather busy. Perhaps we could arrange something more formally…"

Richard Brown still had hold of Miles's hand. He stepped forward and grasped the young man by his elbow with his free hand. His mouth was close to Miles's ear. "Listen laddie, I have flown down from Glasgow this morning to discuss this insult. Now, I am sure that you can spare me half an hour of your valuable time. It would be in your interest to get matters sorted out or things are likely to become unpleasant."

Miles took Richard Brown to a meeting room. He offered his visitor a drink, but it was declined. "Let me just go and get the file," he said.

"Sit down laddie. You don't need the file, you know what this is about," said Richard Brown. "What I have to say won't take long. I am here to deliver a message, not to argue about the whys and wherefores."

He stopped and stared around the room. He was certain that there would be no CCTV, but he had to check before he continued.

"You may not know this, but the man who owns Thistle Steel has something of a reputation. He is grossly offended by the implications of your letter. He is a rather hot-headed individual, but I have convinced him that before he comes at you with all guns blazing, so to speak, that this is a mistake. Now I can see that you are a reasonable man. A family man."

He paused and smiled. "You have probably misunderstood the consequences of rejecting this claim and I have come to appeal to you to reconsider. You have two weeks to change your mind."

Miles started to speak "I think…" but Richard Brown stood up and held out a hand to silence him. He produced a business card from the breast pocket of his Crombie and placed it in the middle of the table. "You can get hold of me here if you need to but, hopefully, that will be unnecessary. I hope to receive the claim cheque shortly. I'll see myself out," he said and picked up his briefcase and headed for the door.

Miles could feel that his legs were shaking. He reached out to pick up the business card. It read: "Richard Brown DipLP, ACCA. Company Secretary. Thistle Steels Ltd." Below was a Glasgow telephone number, presumably an office number.

The dilemma which Miles thought was resolved now came rushing back and occupied his every waking thought. The threat that he had dismissed as the result of his over active imagination had now been demonstrated to him as being distinctly real.

What did Richard Brown mean when he said that Jaimie McGovern wanted to come at him "with all guns blazing." Was it just a figure of speech or should he take it in the literal sense?

He had practical experience of McGovern's potential to use violence and that had been for the equivalent of stepping on the man's foot. Would he be prepared to have somebody shot for £1.3 million? Miles thought that he probably would. And how did Brown know that he was a family man? He had not asked it as a question. It had been a statement of fact and had been accompanied by the type of smile that a snake might give a mouse.

Perhaps he should report the incident to the police? But no direct threats had been made and by the look of his business card this guy Brown had some sort of legal qualification.

Miles thought back to when he had encountered Jaimie McGovern on that drunken night in Glasgow all those years ago. He had called the police then. It had just made matters a hundred times worse. He remembered fleeing through the kitchens and hiding under a blanket in the car that came to rescue him as McGovern's thugs had searched the hotel for him.

The simplest thing to do would be to pay the claim in full: to wash his hands of the matter. But Miles knew that he could not do this. Any claim above £1 million had to be signed off by Giles Smith, Surety and Guarantee's Finance Director. And to do that meant the claim would be further investigated.

How such a large credit limit had come to be written on a company that on paper did not justify it would surely be investigated. And as soon as the investigation found its way to Bill Thompson he was certain to spill the beans. He would tell Giles Smith about the story he heard that day in the golf club. About how Archie Styles had said that Thistle Steel had cheated him before committing suicide.

Giles Smith would come to the same conclusion that Jaimie had. Then Miles would have nowhere to go. He would open himself up to the consequences of the claim being rejected again. He did not like to think of what those consequences might be.

The problem was that Richard Brown did not understand that Miles's authority was limited only to paying a maximum of £1 million. Had he been given a chance he would have explained this, but the man had given him no opportunity to speak. He had simply presented him with an ultimatum, albeit a veiled one, and a time limit. And the clock was already ticking.

Kath noticed that Miles had become withdrawn again. For a couple of weeks, he had seemed to be back to his normal self. But she knew from the number of bottles in the recycling bin that he had resumed drinking heavily. She could tell anyway because she sat next to him on the sofa every night while he stared absently at the screen, his thoughts elsewhere and a large glass of red wine always in his hand. But looking at the number of empty bottles she realised that he must have already drunk one before she sat down. It was while she was upstairs giving Evie a bath and putting her to bed.

Miles had stopped helping with that too. He always seemed to have been drinking before he came home as well. Every night she greeted him with a kiss, but his return kiss was now more perfunctory and with closed lips. That did not stop her smelling the beer on his breath. He had stopped giving Evie a hug too.

One night she suggested to him that he might be depressed and that he should go and see the doctor. Miles had reacted angrily. "Just leave me alone, I am perfectly fine," he had shouted. Kath was only trying to help him, and she resented that he would not let her.

Chapter 20

For a week Miles did nothing. He simply sat and replayed his encounter with Richard Brown trying to decide which course of action was best to take. His conclusions were always the same. It was if he were in a cage and he would roam up and down testing the lock on the door and each steel bar individually to see if any of them gave but knowing that he had done this a hundred times before and that there was simply no way out.

He was scared not only for himself but for Kath and Evie too. If Miles had just been a single man, the solution would have been obvious. He simply would have reported the issue to the Board of Surety and Guarantee and then to the police.

He knew that he could look after himself, but he could not stand the idea of Kath or Evie being used as pawns in a psychopath's game. Increasingly his thoughts turned to suicide. In many ways Miles thought it would be better if he simply removed himself from the equation. If he was dead, then there would be nobody for McGovern to intimidate. Or would there? Thistle Steel's claim would still exist. The problem would just shift to one of his colleagues and their family.

And how would Evie be affected if he killed himself? His own father had died three years before, tranquilly in hospital. His dad, Harry, had set all his affairs straight and made his peace with the world; yet, it had crushed Miles's spirit. It had been six months before he had been able to get some perspective on the situation.

Mike Stott

Even now, he missed Harry terribly and he knew he always would. How on earth would your father committing suicide affect an eight -year old, he thought? It would scar Evie for life and break Kath's heart. No, it was the coward's way out. But Miles still could not think of a better solution.

A line from a play sprang into his head: "Oh that this too, too solid flesh would melt. Thaw and resolve itself into a dew." What was that? Hamlet? Yes, Hamlet he decided. He had studied the play at school. He remembered that Mr. Bowen, his English teacher, had said that the last part of the quote was a pun and that when it was spoken, as it was meant to be, it could mean "a dew," meaning a puddle of water, or the French word for goodbye: "Adieu." Either way it meant the end. An exit from the problems of this world.

Miles left the office at 5 o'clock and walked to the Hydrant pub at the western end of Eastcheap. His colleagues normally were to be found in the pubs around Leadenhall Market, the Lamb Tavern or the New Moon, but he did not want company or conversation.

As he walked to the pub, he noticed that the nights were drawing in. Already it was dusk, and the street lamps and office windows reflected pools of warm light onto the pavement.

He looked at the buildings as he walked. When he had started work in the late 1970s they had been black, and smoke streaked. Now the facades were clean showing the warm brown stone beneath. Over the years all the buildings had been sand blasted and apart from the traffic Miles felt that this part of London would not be unfamiliar to somebody from the time of Charles

Dickens. He walked past Pudding Lane where the Great Fire of London had started in 1666. Everywhere there were reminders of the past in this ancient town.

Starlings were beginning to circle in the sky. He looked up. It was full of cranes. Everywhere new buildings were being erected: vast edifices of stone and glass as a testament to the money that was pouring into the city.

Miles reached the pub. He ordered a pint of Stella and then perched on a seat at the bar. His dilemma would not leave him, but he found that if he drank enough he could sometimes see matters in a better light and, if not, it allowed him a few hours of fitful sleep at least.

Miles listened to the music that was being piped through the pub's speakers. A tune came on that he remembered from long ago. It was "Coward of the County" by Kenny Rogers. As a teenager, he had hated the song with its saccharin lyrics.

He thought about his dad driving him to play football on the pitches at the Jubilee Sports Ground in Lewisham one weekend in the late 1970s. The song had come on the radio and his dad had sung along, nudging him in the ribs to join in when the chorus came on and laughing.

Miles remembered it was a song about a man whose wife was gang raped by three cowboys. A strange topic for Radio 2 on a Sunday morning he thought, particularly as they had denied the Sex Pistols airplay a few years before for saying that the Queen was a fascist.

The song's main theme was that a man had promised his father not to fight. Then one night these men gang raped his wife. His revenge was to lock all three in a room and beat them up. Even at the time Miles thought that was getting off lightly. You should have got 20 years for gang rape and your balls cut off in his opinion.

He listened to the singer's country croon. Before he died his father had looked like Kenny Rogers with a shock of white hair and a white beard. Like Harry, Miles's hair had never receded although it was still mostly brown, with just a touch of grey at the temples. Not like poor old Charlie, Miles thought, he was nearly bald.

He listened to the last chorus of the song, and sang along to it in his head:

"I promised you dad not to do the things you've done
I walk away from trouble when I can
Now please don't think me weak, I didn't turn the other cheek
And papa I sure hope you understand
Sometimes you gotta to fight when you're a man"

Miles wished his dad was still alive. He would have been able to tell him what was going on and he was sure that his father would have been able to help him. Harry had been as brave as a lion.

At 6 o'clock after consuming two more pints he crossed the road to Monument Tube Station. It was only three stops to Liverpool Street, but it had started to rain, and he did not feel like walking.

He stared up at the Doric column erected to commemorate the Great Fire of London. He had walked up to the top once with Kath. He remembered how they had both been out of breath when they reached the viewing platform. He could see his parent's flat from there, he recalled. All the way from the river to Peckham Rye. Turn the other way and you could see St. Paul's. Move round and there was the Millennium

Wheel and the Houses of Parliament. How many steps up were there, 200 perhaps? Maybe he could throw himself off there?

He stood on the escalator as it took him deep below the City of London streets. He turned left and pushed his way to the end of the platform busy with commuters returning to their homes in the suburbs.

Miles stood back from the crowded platform. He looked up at the electronic information board, the letters lit in green. There was a train due in one minute and another one a minute after that.

He heard the first one approaching and noticed as it came into view and the carriages swept past him that they were all extremely full, packed with people eager to get home. He decided to wait for the second train. As an experienced commuter of many years he knew that at least eighty per cent of the people on the platform would try and get on the train currently standing on the platform. They would push other people down the aisles and stand nose to nose for the benefit of saving a valuable sixty seconds. He knew that the second train arriving so quickly afterwards would be half full at best.

When the train pulled away the platform was nearly empty. Miles picked up his briefcase and shuffled towards the edge of the platform. He could hear the second train coming. "The distant echo of far-away voices boarding far-away trains," Paul Weller's plaintive voice sang in his head.

As the Tube train appeared from out of the tunnel Miles felt a tap on his back. He turned, and a hand grasped him around the shoulder. Standing right behind him was a huge man. This close in Miles could not tell how tall he was but the man towered over him.

His accoster leaned in as the train began to slow into the station. "I have a message. You only have seven more days to resolve matters. Please see that you do, or life will become very unpleasant for you and your family."

The man let go of his shoulder and gave him a small shove towards the stopping train. It was not hard enough to push him onto the rails and anyway the train would have now blocked his fall. It was a suggestion of what might happen though. Miles looked again to see the large man disappearing into the passageway that exited the station. He stumbled onto the train and the doors closed behind him.

On the journey home Miles began to think about what had happened to Archie Styles. Bill Thompson had said that he had committed suicide by throwing himself in front of a train; but perhaps it was not suicide? What if Archie had been thrown in front of a train to shut him up? Bill had said that Archie had been telling people that Thistle Steel had cheated him. Perhaps they were worried that he would speak to the Receiver of Gainsborough Steel about it or go to the police? Nobody had said what type of train it was that killed Archie. Pushing someone under a Tube train would not be too difficult, Miles thought. It might be a bit harder with a cross-country express but not impossible.

He must have been followed from the office, Miles mused. His attacker could have chosen to deliver his message anywhere on his way home. The fact that he had waited until a Tube train was arriving at the platform that Miles was standing on was clearly deliberate. And so much for the theory that he was safe due to living a long way from Glasgow. The man had a south London accent like Miles. Jaimie

McGovern's reach was much further than he had expected. Miles knew that had no choice. He had to act.

Chapter 21

Miles arrived at the office early the next day. He had not been able to sleep. He looked tired and drawn and his head ached from the two bottles of wine he had drunk at home while Kath was out with her friends.

After taking his coat off and putting his briefcase by his chair he sat down. He opened the top drawer of his desk and took out Richard Brown's blue and white embossed business card. He looked at the clock. It was only just after a quarter past eight. He decided to leave it for a couple of hours before calling and put the card back in the drawer.

As he sat in a local café eating a bacon sandwich and drinking a can of Coke he rehearsed what he needed to say to Richard Brown. He would have to throw himself on the man's mercy and having already met him he was not sure this would work; but he had to break the deadlock. The events of the previous evening had convinced him that he could not simply sit and do nothing. He needed to appeal to the man's logic; to explain that he could not pay more than a million pounds and that pressing for the full amount would put matters in jeopardy for them both.

Miles went back to the office and tried to busy himself with paperwork until the clock ticked around to half past ten. He opened the drawer in his desk and took out the business card. Carefully he dialled the number printed on it.

"Thistle Steel," a receptionist replied.

"Could I speak to Richard Brown please?" asked Miles.

"Where are you from?" asked the receptionist.

"Surety and Guarantee," replied Miles

"And what is the nature of your call?" said the receptionist, sounding frosty.

"It's about Credit Insurance," said Miles beginning to be frustrated by the interrogation.

"He wouldn't be interested. We already have that," said the receptionist sounding as if she were about to end the call.

"No, wait a minute," said Miles hurriedly. "Thistle Steel already have a policy with us and I am calling to talk about a claim."

"One moment," the receptionist snapped as if she did not believe him. Why on earth do companies give receptionists the power to reject incoming calls? Miles wondered as he waited. The woman had been like some sort of mythical dragon who guarded the gates of a castle.

A voice came on the line: "Richard Brown."

"Mr. Brown, it's Miles Dixon from Surety and Guarantee."

"Yes, I know," said the irritated voice. "Where are you calling me from?"

"From my office," said Miles sounding confused.

"Well, I don't wish to discuss specifics over the telephone. I take it that you have some good news for me?" said Brown.

"Um, yes," Miles stumbled. "But a have a small issue that I need to discuss. It's about…"

"I have told you, not on the telephone," came an exasperated reply.

"Well, can we meet then?" said a flustered Miles.

"Yes. Are you available tomorrow?"

"Yes," agreed Miles.

"Very well, I will see you at your offices at 11 o'clock."
The line went dead.

At precisely 11am the next morning the telephone rang
on Miles' desk. "Mr. Brown in reception to see you,"
said a female voice from the front desk.

Miles caught the lift down to the ground floor. He saw
Richard Brown on the other side of the glass barrier. As
before he was dressed in a dark suit and a Crombie. He
had his hands in the pocket of his coat and was staring
at Miles as he exited the lift. Standing beside his visitor
was a huge man holding a briefcase. He too wore a
dark suit, but it looked like he was unused to dressing
in this manner. His shoes were cheap, pointy and slip-
on. He could not be sure, but it looked like the man
who had accosted him at Monument Tube Station two
days before.

Miles flicked his pass over the electronic reader and the
glass gates opened. He walked towards Richard Brown
his hand extended. "Mr. Brown," he said. His visitor's
hands remained in the pockets of his Crombie. He
looked Miles up and down. "This is Ben," he said
inclining his head towards his sidekick. Ben nodded.
"Get your coat laddie. I want to go somewhere neutral
to talk about this."

Miles had returned to his office to collect his jacket.
The three men exited the Surety and Guarantee
building and walked in single file, led by Ben, to the
Lamb Tavern. It was only 11.15 and the bar was almost
empty. Richard Brown found a table in a corner where
it would be unlikely the conversation would be
overheard.

As Miles sat opposite, he said, "Before we start, I am
going to have to ask you to go to the toilet. Go in the

end cubicle and leave the door unlocked. Ben will join you in a minute." He smiled when he saw the panic on Miles's face. "No need to worry laddie. Big Ben just needs to make sure that you are not recording this conversation."

Miles made his way to the toilet cubicle and a few seconds later Ben joined him. He frisked Miles quickly and professionally in a manner that showed that he had done this many times before. He then took the mobile from Miles's jacket pocket. He switched it off and disconnected the battery before handing it back.

As Miles returned to the seat opposite Richard Brown, Ben went to the bar and ordered three coffees. He brought two of the drinks to the table where Miles and Richard were sitting and then took his own drink and sat two tables away from them, staring around the bar.

"Now, you said on the 'phone that you had some good news for me. Do you have a cheque with you?" Richard Brown began.

Miles shook his head

"I hope you haven't wasted my time Mr. Dixon," he continued. "You would be very stupid to have done that."

Miles explained haltingly how he was only authorised to pay a claim up to £1 million. He had a dry mouth and took frequent sips of his coffee. Eventually his monologue petered out and the room fell silent.

Richard Brown's expression had turned from impassive to grim as he listened. When Miles had finished speaking he sat and thought for a while. He had not foreseen this problem, but he appreciated the dilemma of the young man sitting in front of him. Maybe one million pounds would do? He stood to clear almost twice as much as that anyway and when he had started out that had been the original target. He would have to convince Jaimie though.

He looked up and began to talk. "This had better not be a delaying tactic laddie." It was not a question. Miles shook his head. His eyes were wide, and he looked scared.

"As I said to you, my boss has something of a hair trigger. If I am to convince him of your argument, then I will need to see some goodwill from you."

Richard Brown was keen to secure his position. "I need to see that the one million pounds has been settled. Are you in a position to do that?" Miles nodded. "Now?" Miles nodded again. "Very well, Ben will escort you back to your office. You can write out the cheque and Ben will bring it back here."

"One thing," Miles said swallowing to find saliva to quench his dry mouth. Richard Brown raised his eyebrows in question. "It isn't a good idea for the claim to be settled exactly on one million pounds. It's too obvious. The accountants will see such a round number and they are sure to question it."

Richard Brown looked down. It was a good point. "How much do you suggest?" he said.

"Something like £997,103. It's random and that's what we want."

Brown sat silently again gazing into the middle distance.

"Well in that case to make it up to a million you owe me £2,897 laddie," Richard Brown said. "I will give you six weeks to get it. I want it in cash and Ben will collect it when we are ready."

Miles nodded meekly.

"Now fuck off," Brown said.

Chapter 22

Kath could not understand the change in Miles, but she was so happy to see it. He had come home that night and it was as if the last few weeks had never happened. He had kissed her and hugged Evie before playing tea parties with her, and he hated doing that even when he was in a good mood. He had not been drinking either. His breath did not smell of beer when he walked through the door. He had volunteered to bath Evie and put her to bed. When they both sat down to watch the television and he had disappeared off into the kitchen she was surprised when he reappeared with a bottle of fizzy mineral water instead of the inevitable glass of red wine. Standing in the middle of the room he took a long swig from the green bottle. "What?" he said when he saw her smiling up at him and he smiled back.

Kath had woken in the middle of the night to find Miles gently snoring next to her. I don't know where you have been but it's lovely to have you back, she thought. It was as if he had been reprieved from a death sentence.

Miles started to go into the office earlier. It was to get a seat on the train he told Kath. In reality, he had let his work slip and he needed the extra hours to catch up but everyday he was winning back ground and becoming the conscientious employee and the loving husband and father he had been.

He still worried that someone at Surety and Guarantee, probably Giles Smith, his Finance Director, would turn up one day at his desk asking questions about the large claim made to Thistle Steel. He had not talked to Bill Thompson about it but hoped that he could keep his mouth shut about his suspicions of fraud. Funnily enough, he had not heard any whispers about this at all and yet Bill Thompson was the most indiscreet man he knew unless it suited him not to be. He was aware that Bill had avoided him too. If he walked into the pub or the office canteen and Bill was there he noticed that he always moved away. This suited Miles. He had no wish to tell Bill that he had paid a claim of nearly £1 million.

In Glasgow Richard Brown sat at his office desk and watched as the face of Jaimie McGovern turned puce.
"One fucking million! They owe us £1.3 million. Fucking insurance companies! What a bunch of untrustworthy bastards! I suppose this is the work of some fucking Claims Adjuster is it? I've paid my premium, now I want them to settle in full."
Richard Brown took a breath and surveyed the man in front of him. McGovern's eyes bulged, and blue veins stood out on his thick neck. He knew Jaimie had a reputation as a psychopath but once upon a time it had always been considered; almost cold. These days he flew into rages at the smallest thing and would not listen to reason. Whether it was hubris or the steroids he took since he had taken up bodybuilding he did not know.
Jaimie had been in a bad mood all week anyway. Another stash had been apprehended by the police. It had only been small: three kilos of cocaine. These events were part and parcel of the business. Still, what type of moron drives around with a defective tail light smoking dope when he is delivering three kilos of cocaine? It was not bad luck: it was sloppy.

"Listen Jaimie, it's not like that," he said pressing his palms in the air as if plumping a pillow. He proceeded to tell his boss of Miles Dixon's dilemma. He had some sympathy with the young man. He had delayed paying the claim longer than expected, yes; but once he had realised the situation he was in he had not tried to do anything stupid. He had not called the police or reported the matter to his Board of Directors. He had been respectful and his advice on not paying one million pounds exactly because it would arouse suspicion showed that he wanted this enterprise to succeed.

In Richard Brown's eyes the whole operation had been an enormous success. And yet Jaimie was standing in front of him inviting more scrutiny. The type of scrutiny that could make the whole plan unravel and bring the police to their door. Jaimie was feared but he was also on Glasgow's Most Wanted list. If this went wrong, it could deliver their whole operation to Central Police Headquarters in a box with wrapping paper and a ribbon. Richard Brown put a voice to his thoughts.

After he had finished his plea Jaimie stared at him silently for what was only a few seconds but felt like ten minutes. "You are going soft in your old age," he said eventually. "This lad, Dixon is playing you. We only have his word for it that his authority level is a million pounds. What if he has been told to say that? These people never offer you everything up front, do they? They make you an offer and hope that you say, "thank you" and go away. If you don't and they have to pay in full well then it was always worth a try wasn't it? No," Jaimie shook his head. "No. They owe me another 300k and I want it."

Richard Brown sighed inwardly. There was no point in arguing.

Two weeks later Miles made his usual way up Leadenhall Street to Liverpool Street station. His weekly meeting with Giles Smith had concluded quickly that afternoon. The early morning starts meant that Miles was now up-to-date with his work and he had used it as an excuse to leave half an hour early.

As he crossed the road at the pedestrian crossing, he saw Big Ben standing on the pavement immediately ahead. The man had his arms crossed and was looking directly at him. Miles was surprised. It had only been a fortnight since he put the claims cheque in the man's hand and Richard Brown had said that he had another two weeks to pay the balance. Perhaps he was just checking? It would not be a problem though, using the cash machine at the newsagents by his office, Miles had been taking small amounts every day from his and Kath's saving account. He was hoping that she would not notice if he took it out like that in random amounts. He already had the full balance in an envelope in his briefcase and he was relieved it was there now that he saw Ben staring down at him.

Miles approached Ben who grabbed him around the bicep. He leaned down. "Mr. Brown wants to see you," he said. At their previous meeting Ben had not said a word. Not even as he frisked Miles. Not "thank you" when he had put the envelope with the cheque in his hand or "goodbye" when he had left. Miles recognised the accent. It was south London. It was the same man who had delivered the message to him at Monument tube Station. Ben led him to a doorway. They walked down a flight of steps into an underground wine bar.

Some jazz was playing, and Richard Brown sat at a table that looked like an upturned wooden barrel.

Unlike before Richard Brown felt it unnecessary to search Miles. He had not been expecting his visit, so he would not have come prepared. He did ask him to hand his mobile to Ben though, and again the battery was disconnected. "I know what you are here for," said Miles, putting his briefcase on the table lid and flipping the locks. He pulled out an envelope and handed it to Richard Brown who accepted it with his thumb and forefinger as if he had been handed a dog turd. After peering into the envelope, he put the package into the inside pocket of his Crombie. "It's all there," said Miles hoping that would conclude the meeting and, indeed, these matters forever.

"I am sure it is," said Richard Brown calmly. "I delivered your claim's cheque to my boss. Unfortunately, he feels that you are holding back on him. He thinks you owe him another three hundred thousand pounds."

Miles looked stunned. It was like he had negotiated a path out of a maze and turned a corner expecting to see an exit and open countryside beyond and instead being confronted by a giant hedge of thorns towering in front of him. He put his hand across his forehead. "I can't get you another 300k. I would if I could, honestly, but it's impossible."

Richard Brown looked at him sympathetically. "Listen laddie, I am just the messenger here, I thought we had a deal too, but it won't wash. You are an intelligent man, I am sure that you can work something out. There must be ways and means to do this," he paused. "I'm sorry but if you can't deliver it won't be me you are dealing with. What comes next will be much nastier, I urge you to find a way. You have two weeks. You know where to find me." He nodded at Ben and then stood up and walked out closely followed by his minder.

Miles stood up unsteadily. He walked to the bar and returned to the table with a beer. He needed time to think. Richard Brown might be right, there may be an answer to paying out another £300k. He thought quietly taking long glugs at his pint and getting up to get another when that was finished.

Could he get Richard Brown to set up another company and take out another policy, so he did not have to pay another claim to Thistle Steel? He rejected the idea. Setting up a new company was the work of minutes but setting up a new policy would take too much time. Miles was not responsible for selling policies anyway and had no access to the department that issued the paperwork. If not that way, then could he pay the money as part of another claim? In as much time as it took to think of the idea he dismissed it. Large claims had to be confirmed by the insolvency practitioner.

Miles drank two more pints. He could not come up with any better way than simply paying the claim in the same way as he had paid the last one. He would have to take the chance that nobody noticed it.

He looked at his watch. Christ, it was 7.40! He would not be home much before nine o'clock. He needed to call Kath. He reached in the pocket of his jacket for his mobile and discovered that he had forgotten to reconnect the battery. He pushed the two pieces of the 'phone together. There was no signal down there. He picked up his briefcase and headed for the door. As he walked up the stairs his 'phone began to ping as the mobile telephone signal found him. He looked at the screen. He had eight missed calls from Kath and three from Charlie. His 'phone pinged again: and five voicemails.

Chapter 23

Miles did not bother to check the voicemails. Clearly something was urgent. He pressed Kath's mobile number on his speed dial. It was answered immediately.

"Miles? Where the fuck have you been?" Kath said. She sounded hysterical and she was crying.

"I know I'm late love. I'm sorry. I'll be home soon."

"Miles, I'm at the police station, "sobbed Kath. Miles's heart went cold. Not Evie. Please not Evie. "I've been robbed."

Kath worked part-time as an administrative assistant for a firm of financial advisers in Romford town centre. The job allowed her to drop Evie off at school in the mornings and be back to pick her up from after school club at 5pm each evening.

As usual, she had left work at 4.45 and made her way through the dimly lit car park behind the offices. Because she was always the last one to arrive in the morning, she always had to park the furthest away and that part of the car park was quiet and dark, particularly as the clocks had gone back the week before.

She was not aware of being followed. Perhaps the man who sprang out behind her had been hiding behind a parked car? He had pinned her against the fence, his elbow and forearm pushed against her neck and a giant hand covering the side of her face that was turned towards him.

She had not seen what he looked like and was only aware of a leather-gloved hand pressing on her mouth, nose and eye. She whimpered. "Shut the fuck up," said the man. The accent was local: Essex. With his other hand he had taken the handbag, which was hanging from a strap over her arm and lifted out her purse, which he flipped open and looked inside before pocketing it. "Now you haven't seen me, "he said pushing her face harder into the fence. "And remember, I know where you live."

How did he know that? Kath panicked. Maybe, he had seen the driving licence in the windowpane section of her purse? She felt a sharp jab in her back and collapsed as her attacker turned away and moved hurriedly off. She lay for a few minutes crying quietly. Her lower back ached. She felt it with her hand. She could not feel any blood. He must have just punched her.

After a while she had pulled herself up using the wing mirror of a parked Toyota. She bent down to retrieve her upturned handbag and unsteadily made her way back to the office, leaning on the parked cars as she went.

As she re-entered her work premises all her colleagues looked up from their desks and stared at her. She must have looked a sight. He white Burberry raincoat was wet and stained where she had lain in a puddle in the car park. The side of her face, which had been pushed into the fence, was stinging too like it had been grazed.

Very soon she found herself sitting down surrounded by concerned faces. Sue, her friend, handed her a cup of tea. She sipped at it and made a face. "I put six sugars in it," said Sue. "It's for shock. Drink it."

Kath got halfway through telling the story of her attack when she realised that Evie would be waiting for her. She looked in her handbag for her mobile, afraid that her attacker had taken that too. Then with relief she remembered that she had left it in the pocket of her raincoat, which was now drying over a chair next to the radiator.

She could not help thinking that the attacker had not been very thorough. He had taken her purse but that only had a debit card and a credit card in, both of which Sue was on the telephone cancelling. There was also about forty pounds in cash. Not much for that type of robbery. Maybe he had not attacked her to rob her? Maybe it was a sex attack, but he had changed his mind for some reason?

Kath retrieved the mobile from her coat pocket. She tried to call Miles. No answer. She tried again and left a message this time. She looked at her watch. Her attacker didn't try to take that either, she thought, and this one was expensive: it was a Rado that Miles had bought her for their tenth wedding anniversary.

It was 5.26. She called the after-school club and explained quickly what had happened. The person that answered said that she would be there until 6.30 and would call Kath back if nobody had been to pick Evie up by then.

Kath called Miles again. Still no answer. She left another voicemail. Then she called Miles's office. She spoke to Rob Hatton, Miles's deputy. He told her that her husband had left about half an hour before and when questioned said that to the best of his knowledge he was on his way home.

Exasperated and upset, Kath finally called Charlie. He worked at a local Kwikfit. After swearing about junkie scumbags, he said that he would collect Evie and take her back to his house and that he would keep calling Miles. Kath finished her call and looked up to see two policemen enter the building. Sue must have called them.

Miles arrived home just after nine o'clock. He was out of breath as he had run most of the way from the railway station.

Kath had been taken to the local police station and had given a statement and a description of the attacker, which was extremely vague. They seemed to agree with Charlie that it was an addict getting money to score. He had not seemed like that to Kath. In fact, she remembered that he smelled of an expensive aftershave. Did junkies wear aftershave?

When she had finished the two policemen offered her a lift home, but Kath had insisted on being taken back to her car and had then picked up Evie from Charlie's. She had not long settled her daughter down in bed when Miles returned. He looked flushed and she did not think it was just that he had been running.

"Are you okay love?" Miles asked. He approached and tried to hug her. She could smell the beer on his breath. She pushed him away.

"Where have you been Miles?" she asked coldly.

"I had to finish something off, so I did not leave until late," he replied looking hurt at her rejection.

"Until now? Come on. And why didn't you answer your phone?"

Miles looked flustered. "When I finished I went for a drink. It was one of those underground wine bars. I didn't realize but there was no 'phone signal. I lost track of the time. I'm sorry. It was Rob Hatton's birthday."

Kath sighed. She was too tired to fight.

Miles did not sleep that night. When he had finally returned Kath's call earlier that evening she had explained to him that the police had thought the motive behind the attack was drugs. Kath did not agree with their conclusion and neither did he. The attacker had taken very little. It was almost a token robbery designed to deliver a threat to him; designed to ensure his co-operation.

The timing was right too. Richard Brown would have known there was no mobile signal in the wine bar, besides they had taken the battery out of his mobile. Unusually Ben had left them for a couple of minutes and gone back up the stairs towards the street, Miles remembered. Had he contacted the attacker to tell him that the coast was clear?

The whole purpose seemed to be to convince Miles that whatever problems he faced in paying the extra three hundred thousand pounds they would be as nothing compared to the consequences of not paying it. He concluded that he needed to address the problem the next day.

Miles arrived at the office early. Kath was not talking to him and she seemed angry. Maybe the psychological effects of the previous evening's attack had begun to hit her? He thought that maybe she would take the day off, but she had got up showered and dressed for the office and got Evie ready for school. His dad had always said that Kath was made of stern stuff, and he was right.

Miles had left the house without eating breakfast to avoid the frosty atmosphere. Besides, he needed to grasp this nettle. One final act and he would be free.

He waited until just after nine o'clock before making the call to Richard Brown. Miles hoped that he had returned to Glasgow on the late flight the night before. The call was answered. This time he explained to the receptionist that Mr. Brown was expecting to hear from him. The call was put straight through.

"Mr. Brown, good morning, it's Miles Dixon," He heard a perfunctory acknowledgement. "I am ready to settle the final part of your claim in full. How would you like me to transfer the money?"

"Have a cheque made out as before," came the reply. "I will collect it some time in the next few days. I take it that you will be in the office this week?" Miles agreed that he would. "Have the cheque ready please," came the reply and the line was disconnected.

Later that afternoon the telephone rang on the desk. "Mr. Brown is here to see you Miles," came the receptionist's voice. Miles looked at his watch. It was 3.20pm. He must have left Thistle's office straight after their telephone conversation.

Miles opened his desk and took out the envelope containing the cheque he had made out to Thistle Steel that morning. To avoid suspicion, once again he had avoided the round number of three hundred thousand pounds and instead made it out for £299, 974. If Richard Brown insisted on the deficit being paid then at least it would be only £26: his savings account had been pretty much cleaned out by making up the balance on the last claim.

Miles picked up his jacket and told Rob Hatton that he was going for an off-site meeting with a client. He took the lift down to reception. Once more, Richard Brown was accompanied by Big Ben. As Miles walked towards him he gestured towards Surety and Guarantee's revolving entrance door. As before, the three men made their way to the Lamb Tavern and Ben took Miles straight to the men's toilets to search him.

When he had been thoroughly frisked and his mobile's battery disconnected Miles made his way to where Richard Brown was sitting studying the menu. He took out the envelope containing the claim's cheque and pushed it across the table.

"As you can see it's pretty much in full," Miles said as Brown inspected the cheque. "I have not made it out exactly for £300k as I don't want the auditors looking at it too closely. I had the cheque made out this morning, although I wasn't expecting to see you so quickly."

"Well, I wouldn't like any accidents to befall you while you still owed me this," Richard Brown smiled waving the cheque. "I have to say that given our conversation last night you seem to have overcome your problems very quickly," he added.

Miles explained his thinking process and his decision simply to settle the claim and hope that it would not be investigated any further.

Richard Brown was quiet for a minute pondering what he had just been told. He lifted his head and spoke directly to Miles. His voice was slow and measured. "I hope that concludes business between us Miles, I really do." It was the first time he had referred to Miles by his Christian name.

"You have been very sensible in the way that you have handled matters. It has made life easy for me but also easy for you. If, however, this matter is investigated at some point in the future I would urge you not to lead anybody to my door. It would unleash a response which would bring you more pain than you can imagine. My boss is vindictive. He will see to it that it is not only you that suffers. He will bring suffering to your family and will ensure that you witness it before he exacts his retribution on you.

"Whatever price you must pay in the future to avoid implicating him will be worth it. This is not a threat young man, it is good advice and you should heed it."

He stood up and extended his hand. Miles took it. With his other hand Brown reached up and patted his shoulder, almost in a fatherly way.

Chapter 24

Seven weeks had elapsed, and Miles had begun to think that he was in the clear.

Having the Thistle claim investigated was a fear, which he awoke with every day, but it was a much easier burden to carry than that of the threat of violence to Kath and Evie.

In recent days he had decided that he would leave Surety and Guarantee. That way if a discrepancy was discovered in the future they would have trouble questioning him directly about his role in the matter. They could always involve the police he supposed but it was unlikely. Insurance companies and banks did not like the publicity matters like this brought. They did not like to admit they were vulnerable: it affected the share price.

Miles felt sure that he could easily find another job. Good claims people were hard to come by. There were half a dozen competitors that would fight for his wealth of experience plus a growing bank of specialist brokers that operated in the market. Yes, he would look for a new job in the New Year, he resolved.

The first sign of trouble came on the day of the Christmas party. It was 13th December and the office closed an hour early on that Friday. The theory was that hour was granted so that the staff could get changed before being bussed to a smart hotel in Canary Wharf. The practice was that the women got changed and made themselves ready for the evening's festivities while the men went to the pub for an hour: a pre-drinks ritual which ensured they would be well on their way to drunken abandon by the time they arrived at the venue.

Miles was standing alone at the bar of the Sea Lion. He was taking the first sip of a fresh pint of Guinness when he saw Bill Thompson approaching. Bill looked wary and gave a nod but there was no accompanying insult. The pub was noisy.

Bill stopped and stood very close. "Good to see you Miles. I have been wanting to speak to you for a few days but talking to you in the office is difficult so I'm glad you're here," he began. "Giles Smith has started asking questions about Thistle Steel. He told me a big claim had been paid: £1.3 million, is that right?"

Miles went cold. The numbing effect of the two pints he had already drunk was nullified by the adrenaline that pumped into his bloodstream. "He asked me how an insured limit of that size had come to be written. I took him through the figures and explained that James McDonald had added the top up cover. I don't know how. Maybe he did that off his own bat knowing that he had another job lined up? These salesmen will do anything to earn their commission, you know what they're like? Then they get a job somewhere else and leave us with the mess to clear up."

Miles nodded hoping that the blame would be laid at the door of the now departed James McDonald. "Anyway, just to say that I have not mentioned anything about the story I heard in the golf club concerning Archie Styles. I'm guessing that you checked it out and there was no reason to deny the claim?"

Bill Thompson had decided that Giles Smith had already come to his own conclusions about the Thistle Steel case. James McDonald leaving and joining Surety and Guarantee's main competitor meant that he could pin the blame for the top up cover on him. He was keen though that the matter was not further investigated with the chance that it would uncover his true role. Securing Miles Dixon's silence on the question of the potential fraud was in his interest.

Miles nodded. It had not occurred to him that if Thistle Steel was investigated they would look at why the insured limit had been written. He was relieved to hear that Bill Thompson had kept silent about the fraud. "Yes, I suggest we forget all about the Archie Styles business Bill. It was a red herring. I certainly won't mention it, you have my word on that."

Bill Thompson gave Miles a satisfied smile. "Want another pint wanker?" he asked noticing that his companion had downed his Guinness in the two minutes he had been talking to him. Fucking piss artist, he thought.

The weekend had been an uncomfortable one for Miles Dixon. On the bus to the Christmas party he thought about the conversation with Bill Thompson. The Financial Director, Giles Smith, was aware that the whole claim of £1.3 million had been settled. He was not investigating the claim for nearly £1 million or the second claim for nearly £300k. He had put two and two together and arrived at £1.3 million.

Miles drank heavily that night trying to dismiss his worries, but it was clear he had exceeded his authority. At the party he had noticed Giles Smith sitting at a table in the corner talking to the Chairman. Miles had caught his eye and seen him look away.

The following day Miles had got up late and spent the rest of the day going over what he would say if he was called in to explain the claim. He had already considered his defence. In fact, he had thought of little else over recent weeks, but his mind constantly played out the inevitable inquisition, refining his answers and honing his story.

Matters had not been made better by Kath. Miles had promised to take Evie to her Saturday morning ballet lesson but when his wife had surveyed his red-eyes and smelled his gluey breath she had judged that he was too drunk to drive. When she came home with Evie she had shouted at Miles saying that his drinking was out of control and that he was selfish. He lay on the sofa for the rest of the day worrying and feeling sorry for himself.

On Monday Miles arrived at the office early. If it had not been for the thought of his impending encounter with Giles Smith he would have glad to have been at work. Since shouting at him on Saturday Kath had ignored him for the rest of the weekend. He had felt ashamed of himself.

The day passed slowly but at 5 o'clock as he left the building Miles felt more optimistic. Maybe the whole issue had been kicked under the carpet with the blame laid to rest at the door of the now unimpeachable James McDonald? It would not be the first time he had seen the company blame an absent scapegoat, particularly where the responsibility for the fuck-up lay with the senior management. Some of the Directors could dodge punches better than the young Muhammad Ali.

On the way back from the station he bought Kath some flowers and stopped off at a toyshop to buy a new outfit for Evie's Barbie.

It was on Thursday that the summons came. The secretary to the Directors came to Miles desk and asked Miles to accompany her to the Board Room where the Finance Director wanted to see him. Miles grabbed his jacket and put it on as he walked behind her. She did not try to talk to him.

When he entered room with it's long mahogany table and plate glass window overlooking the City Miles noticed that the room was not only occupied by Giles Smith but also the Personnel Director and his assistant.

The accusations against Miles were much as he expected. He had exceeded his authority and had sought to disguise it. Miles began to speak but the Personnel Director held up his hand to silence him.

"This is a preliminary meeting," he said. "A full disciplinary meeting will take place on Monday, here at 3pm. The Board of Directors regard your actions as being Gross Misconduct and, as such, this is a dismissible offence without the requirement for three written warnings if we consider your actions to have exceeded your level of authority." The man would not meet Miles's gaze. Instead, he addressed the shiny table.

"You are entitled to be legally represented or to bring in a friend or adviser. My assistant will now escort you from the building and you are required to hand your swipe card to her. You are not required to work between now and the disciplinary hearing and, indeed, access to the building or to your computer is denied."

Miles went home. He had decided not to tell Kath of that afternoon's events. The next day he told Kath that he was not feeling well and that he was not going to work. "Well, you should drink less," she scowled. The flowers had not really helped. He was keen not to get into a fight and offered to take Evie to school and pick her up so that she would not have to go to after school club. "Okay," Kath nodded and gave him a thin smile as she left the house. "I hope you feel better."

Evie's school was only a ten-minute walk and it was quicker to walk than to drive. The traffic was usually nose-to-tail and the double yellow lines on the road outside the school were always covered in SUV vehicles with their hazard lights flashing.

Miles walked along the pavement while Evie skipped through the frosty grass on the verges leaving small white footprints. She was singing as she skipped "When Santa got stuck up the chimney, he began to shout." It was her school Christmas concert next week and she had been practising this new song. She had not seemed to notice the fraught atmosphere at home between her parents.

Evie stopped by the lollipop lady at the school crossing and waited for her father to catch up.

Miles and Evie stood and waited patiently as the lollipop lady stuck out her sign and edged nervously into the road. A white 7-series BMW pulled to a stop and they began to cross. The driver gave a friendly pip-pip on his horn. Miles looked through the windscreen expecting to see one of Evie's friends' parents. Big Ben was smiling at him.

Between dropping Evie off and going back to pick her up Miles spent the day worrying. If Surety and Guarantee were investigating the Thistle Steel claim had they been in touch with Richard Brown? Was that why Big Ben had turned up? Or was it just a coincidence? There seemed to be too many coincidences. Was Kath being attacked a coincidence?

At 3.30 Miles stood outside the school gates. "Daddy!" Evie shouted excitedly as she came through the school door. She ran towards him. He squatted down to pick her up, stood straight and swung her round in his arms. As he turned Miles saw Big Ben. He was about fifty yards away standing motionless on the pavement looking in his direction. Ben raised his finger to his lips then turned and walked away.

Miles sat in the reception of Surety and Guarantee waiting to be escorted to the Board Room. He had not bothered to get legal representation. He did not think that George Carmen could get him off this one. It would have been an expensive bill that he could ill-afford and it would not change the outcome.

He had not thought about being accompanied by one of his work colleagues either. The Directors would be keen to cover this matter up and that suited Miles too. He did not want the details of this enquiry being shared in the pubs of Fenchurch Street by some blabbermouth from the third floor.

He was led up to the Boardroom by the silent secretary. The meeting was almost the same as the week before with the exception that Miles was allowed to speak in defence of his actions. He explained that the reason he had paid the claim in two instalments was that there had been that there had been some possibility that some of Thistle's stock could be recovered, which had reduced their claim to below £1 million. "It had then become clear that no recoveries had been made thus making it necessary to make a second payment, "he explained.

"Miles, we have investigated your file and your computer over the weekend. There is nothing to suggest what you say is true. In fact, no notes were made at all between the payment of the first claim and the payment of the second. But, if what you say is true then you still needed my approval for the second payment," said the Giles Smith.

"I forgot," Miles mumbled. The Financial Director shook his head.

The meeting was adjourned for twenty minutes while his interrogators consulted. Miles was taken to an empty office ad left to stare out of the window.

When the meeting resumed it was the Personnel Director who spoke: "Mr. Dixon after consultation we have decided that you have exceeded your authority and that your actions constitute Gross Misconduct.

You have worked here for many years and I am sure you understand that we must take this matter extremely seriously. Your argument that you forgot to get the second claim sanctioned by the Finance Director is simply unacceptable. As a result of this you are dismissed with immediate effect. You will be paid up to today's date. My assistant will now escort you from the building and if you have any valuables or personal items in your desk you can arrange with her to put them in a box for your collection."

Miles rose, but the Financial Director started to speak, and he sat down again. "Miles, I am terribly disappointed with you. Quite honestly, I don't understand what has happened to you. There is nothing in the files to suggest this but if I find that you have been in collusion with the client and benefitted financially in any way, I will refer this matter to the police."

Giles Smith had no intention of reporting this matter to the police. The Board of Directors had decided that bad publicity was something that they did not need. Still, he had endured a very uncomfortable half hour being scrutinised by his fellow directors and he was determined to have his pound of flesh. If it gets out it will be an example to the others, he thought.

Miles made his way down Leadenhall Street. The Christmas lights were starting to come on as it became dark. The shop windows glittered with tinsel and artificial snow and the decorations on a large spruce tree in the plaza in front of the Gherkin building flashed.

The next day was Christmas Eve. He thought of a reformed Ebenezer Scrooge leaning from his window and telling a boy to go and buy the biggest turkey in the market. As he passed a pub doorway he could hear Elvis Presley singing "Blue Christmas."

Chapter 25

"Redundant! They made you redundant two days before Christmas?" Kath was angry and upset.

Miles shrugged. Her could not tell her the truth. He realised that despite having paid Thistle's fraudulent claim and losing his job he still had a secret burden to bear. To share the real reason with Kath was to invite her to go to the police or to share with him the worry of keeping silent.

"They said they were shedding quite a few people, I suppose that once they started handing out redundancy notices they thought the news would spread anyway," he lied.

"Still at Christmas for fuck's sake," said a teary Kath.

"Never mind," said Miles trying to look optimistic. "There are plenty of jobs out there. We'll have a good Christmas and in the New Year I'll start looking. I have been at Surety and Guarantee too long anyway. I have got stuck in my ways. This is probably the kick in the arse I needed."

Kath nodded and looked brighter. "What about redundancy pay? You have been there a long time, it must be quite a bit."

Again, Miles shrugged. "They said they would let me know."

"Even if it's only statutory redundancy pay it is something like one week's wages for every year worked," Kath said. "You have been there for over twenty-five years. It should be easily enough to see us through for the next six months, you will have found a new job by then. Maybe it will be a lot more than that? We could go to Florida at Easter."

Evie bounced into the room. Her eyes glittered with the reflected light from the Christmas tree. "Father Christmas is coming! He's nearly here," she said excitedly and bounced down onto the sofa next to Miles. He reached out and pulled here closer to him, kissing her head. "Well, there's one good thing: I don't have to go back to work on the 27th," he smiled at Kath. "Yes. Let's forget about it until after Christmas," she agreed.

Miles worked on his CV over the Christmas period. It was very short: 3 O Levels, 5 months at Sainsbury's and 28 years at Surety and Guarantee. Still, he reasoned, he had worked in every department of his old employer. Experience like his was hard to come by.

In the New Year he registered with a specialist recruitment agency in the City. They invited him in for an informal chat as soon as they received his CV in the post and the consultant that he saw seemed very enthusiastic about his prospects.

He had got around the difficult question of why he had left his former role by citing personal differences with his immediate superior, Giles Smith. Miles hoped that on that basis the need for a reference would be waived.

Within a few days they had lined up an interview with Surety and Guarantee's largest competitor. The role was at Director level and the money and benefits that were being offered were considerably better than at his previous employer. Kath was excited when he told her. Maybe the recruitment consultant had been right when he said that eventually all companies will treat you as part of the furniture if you stay too long?

Miles attended his first interview the following week. It was with the Personnel Director of Credit Indemnity PLC.

The meeting lasted well over an hour and it went so well that he was not surprised to be invited back for a second interview with the Managing Director the following week. At the end of that interview he was told that his application had been successful and subject to a medical examination he could start at the beginning of February. When he told Kath, she began talking excitedly about booking a holiday to Florida.

It was the following week while Miles was taking Evie to the park that the recruitment agency called him on his mobile. It was explained that Credit Indemnity had applied to Surety and Guarantee for a reference and what they had learned meant that they were retracting their job offer. Miles felt like he had been punched.

"As a result of this we have also conducted our own investigations into the circumstances leading to you leaving your previous employer," the recruitment consultant continued. "We are very disappointed at having been misled over this matter and as a result we will be removing you as a candidate for any further vacancies," he concluded.

It seemed that the whole of the Credit Insurance market was aware of the circumstances of Miles Dixon's sacking. He applied through several other agencies and began sending out his CV directly but there were no further offers forthcoming. It seemed that Giles Smith's spiteful nature had gone into overdrive. He had wondered why none of his former colleagues had been in touch. Now, he knew. Even widening his net to apply for jobs in general insurance or credit reporting agencies yielded nothing.

Money was becoming a problem too. Jobseeker's Allowance was a paltry £69 a week and apart from the Children's Allowance for Evie that was all the Dixon's as a family were entitled to. Kath's sympathy had turned into incomprehension when the job offer was withdrawn. Her frustration had quite quickly turned to resentment.

Matters finally came to a head one Thursday evening in April. Kath had returned home. Miles had shouted down a greeting from his office upstairs as he heard her come through the door. There was no reply. He walked down the stairs.

Kath was standing in the kitchen waiting for the kettle to boil so that she could make a cup of tea. "Everything okay love?" he asked. Kath slapped him. It was hard and unexpected, and the side of his face was stinging from the blow.

"I went to Sainsbury's at lunchtime to do some shopping," she said. Miles furrowed his brow. Why had she just hit him and then said something so innocuous as that? How did that justify slapping him?

"When I got to the till my credit card was rejected. It was so embarrassing. I had to leave all the shopping behind. When I got back to the office I called Visa and they said that the card was up to its credit limit. So, I checked our bank account. We are overdrawn. What happened to your redundancy money Miles?" Kath's was trying to modulate her voice, but Miles could hear her anger.

"I thought that you had gone quiet about it. I rang up Rob Hatton and asked if the other people who were made redundant were still waiting for their money too. He said that that you weren't made redundant. You were sacked. That's why Credit Indemnity withdrew their offer isn't it? That's why you can't find another job: because you can't get a fucking reference!" She was beginning to shout.

"And you have taken all the money out of our savings account too. A couple of hundred quid here and there until it had all gone. I can only think of three reasons: women, gambling, or drugs. I spoke to the Personnel Department. They wouldn't tell me why they had sacked you but it's one of those isn't it? That's why nobody else wants to take you on."

Miles had begun to cry. "It's not like that Kath. It isn't, I swear."

"Well, tell me what you were sacked for then?" She was suddenly calm and staring straight into his eyes.

Miles stood and thought. Perhaps he should just come clean? Evie walked into the kitchen. She looked up at him and a tear dropped from his eye onto her face. "I can't Kath," he sobbed. Evie hugged his knees.

Chapter 26

The doorbell rang. Sharon Dixon picked up the television remote control and turned the volume down. She was watching" EastEnders" on the BBC and, as usual, the characters were bellowing at each other. It certainly wasn't the East End she knew.

She had been brought up in Bethnal Green just after the war. In those days people got on and tried to help each other. Her parents had seen five years of bombing. First the Luftwaffe during the Blitz, and then the doodlebugs at the end of the war. After that there were years of food shortages with rationing continuing well into the 1950s.

People wanted a quiet life. Yes, the fellas belted each other, usually on a Saturday night after a bellyful of beer. But they shook hands afterwards and got on with it. It cleared the air, as Harry used to say. And he should know, at one time or another he had ended up thumping nearly all his mates. But he was right; they had always carried on being mates afterwards.

She made her way to the door, opened it and peered through the crack, the safety chain still on. Miles was standing on the landing of the flats a holdall at his feet.

"Hello mum. Kath has thrown me out. Can I stay with you?" Sharon unlocked the security chain and held the door open as Miles walked past her and into the living room. The gas fire was on and the place was warm and cosy, just as it used to be when he was a kid.

"Do you want a cup of tea love?" she asked.

"Yes please," Miles nodded. It was mum's answer to everything.

He looked out of the window. The whole place was in a much better state of repair than when he lived there. Instead of abandoned old wrecks in the car park there were now new BMWs and Audis.

There had been squatters in some of the flats when he was a kid; not any more. Apart from his mum's place the rest of flats in the block were now privately owned. The tenants had taken advantage of the Right to Buy scheme started by Margaret Thatcher in the 1980s and with it had come new front doors and smart curtains. Double glazed windows had replaced the old metal casements that used to run with condensation in the winter, pooling on Miles's windowsill and dripping on his head as he lay in his bed underneath.

Only his dad hadn't been tempted to buy his flat from the council. "They are selling back to us what we already own," he snarled when he read of the privatisations of the gas, electricity, water and telephone companies.

Miles remembered the "Tell Sid" television advertisement campaign to encourage people to buy British Gas shares. "Tell Sid that the greedy bastards are lining up to taker their thirty pieces of silver and then we can charge the suckers what we like," Harry had shouted at the TV. "Who's paying for this advert anyway?" he said asking the television a supplementary and largely rhetorical question. "Gercha!" Harry concluded when he had received no answer. Miles had only ever heard Chaz and Dave say "Gercha" before on that beer advert.

His dad had hated Margaret Thatcher. In fact, it was the thing that he usually ended up fighting with his mates about. For the Essex boys of Smithfield Market her philosophy had fitted in with their straightforward view of the world. Not for Harry though. "Posh cow," he would say.

Miles remembered when metal fences had been erected around the Den to stop pitch invasions from the fans. "This is her doing," Harry would say. "She treats working people like animals. If it was down to her she would ban football all together." In the light of the Hillsborough disaster a few years later he had been right.

Miles remembered watching the 1984 miner's strike on the television news with his father and the pictures of policemen with horses and batons charging into lines of pickets. Harry had hated Arthur Scargill as much as he had hated Margaret Thatcher, but he had become incensed by the images. "It's like her own private army," he would rant. "Monetarism isn't the only thing she has borrowed from Chile." Harry had much the same opinion of Thatcher's successor, John Major, too: "Stupid bastard, I can't believe he's from Brixton."

Miles turned away from the window as he heard his mother coming back into the room carrying two cups of tea. She put them both on the coffee table and sat down looking up at her son with a sympathetic smile: a silent invitation for him to speak.

Miles had not told his mum about losing his job, but he did now. He omitted to tell her the reason why he lost it though. He just said that he had been made redundant. He went on to tell her about how he couldn't find another decent job, how money had got tight, how Kath had begun to resent him and how they had started to fight.

"We can't live together anymore. The atmosphere in the house is toxic. It's upsetting Evie too much to see us both behaving like that. He was silent for a minute. "I feel I have let everybody down," he said wiping at his eye.

"You haven't let me down," said Sharon stridently. "I'm proud of you. And I'm proud of Charlie. A woman couldn't have asked for two better sons. Your dad would have been proud of you too. You've looked after everybody. You always have. Your dad used to say that if there was ever a man prepared to take a bullet it was you. You protect people. You've certainly looked after me since your dad has been gone."

His mum had been on her own now for three years. Harry had not long retired when he started complaining about a blister on the heel of his foot. "It's a verruca I think. Don't half hurt though," he had said. Soaking his foot in a bowl of hot salty water and rubbing surgical spirit on it each night had not made a difference.

After a few weeks Sharon had made an appointment for him to see his GP. Harry hated going to the doctors. "Those waiting rooms are full of sick people," he used to say. "You can catch all sorts sitting in those and yet when you first came in there was fuck all wrong with you."

The doctor had said that it was an ulcer linked to the late onset diabetes that Harry had been diagnosed with a few years before. He had dressed the leaking wound and arranged for a District Nurse to visit Harry once a week at home to change the dressings. This had continued for several months with the nurse visiting every Tuesday afternoon.

One day though, a different nurse turned up. She said that the regular District Nurse was on holiday. As she unwrapped the bandage from Harry's foot she started to look concerned. "Everything alright love?" asked Harry. "Oh yes," she smiled.

The next day though, the GP turned up at the front door. Harry had never seen a doctor come out on a house call before, especially unannounced. Even when he had what turned out to be pneumonia and could barely get out of bed and Sharon had pleaded for a doctor to visit the receptionist had insisted that he get a taxi to the surgery.

The doctor had examined the ulcer, then his leg and then poked around in his groin. "It's probably nothing," he said "but I need to arrange a hospital appointment in the next few days. My secretary will arrange it and give you a call. Is there someone who can take you?"

"Yes, I should be able to manage that. It's my diabetes playing up is it doc?" Harry said.

"Probably," said the doctor and smiled thinly.

An appointment was made for that Friday. Sharon had wanted to accompany Harry, but he had insisted that Miles took him. "No problem dad, I work at home most Fridays anyway," he had said when his father telephoned him.

When they arrived in the hospital waiting room Miles was surprised about how quickly the specialist had called Harry in. His only experience of hospitals was waiting in A&E for hours with a football injury or the time he had sat up half the night with Evie when she had tripped over in the garden and fractured her wrist.

Harry and Miles were shown into a small room with an examination couch in one corner. After making sure that he was treating the right patient the specialist

204

asked Harry to remove his trousers and climb up on the couch. Like the GP two days before the specialist unwrapped the dressing and inspected Harry's heel and then his leg. "I'm just going to inspect your groin," he said.

"Miles, go and get yourself a coffee. You don't want to be looking at your old man's meat and potatoes. Go on, and I'll see you in there when we have finished."

Miles had made his way to the hospital café. Fifteen minutes later his father had appeared. "Is everything okay dad?"

"Yes son, right as rain. Nothing to worry about," said Harry.

Over the next few weeks each time he visited Miles noticed that Harry had got thinner and that his eyes and skin looked yellow. "He used to eat like a horse. Now he can't finish what I put in front of him," his mum said.

A few days later Miles took a call from his mum in his office. She said that Harry could not get out of bed and seemed "funny." "I will come straight 'round mum," Miles said. "I think you should call the doctor no matter what dad says." He ended the call and then dialled Charlie.

Harry was sitting up in his hospital bed when Miles walked in. "Hello son. You've just missed your mother," he said.

Miles pulled a plastic chair from the pile on the opposite side of the ward, brought it over to the bedside and sat down. "How are you dad?" Miles had spoken to the doctors almost every time he had visited but they still seemed to be mystified by Harry's illness. Each time they said that they were still conducting tests. His dad looked weak. His cheeks and eyes were sunken.

"Listen son, I'm glad you came. You can see things aren't getting better. In fact, things are going downhill rapidly so I need to tell you now: I've got cancer."

Miles felt like he had been punched. He felt tears well in his eyes. "When did they tell you that?" he asked his voice breaking.

"When we came in that day to see the specialist. I told them not to tell you," said Harry softly. Miles looked stunned.

"Don't be angry with me son. That thing on my foot was skin cancer not an ulcer. God knows how it got there but the specialist said these things spread rapidly if they are not picked up quickly and I have had this for months. He said there were lumps in my groin and it would already have spread to other organs. It's in my liver, that's why I'm yellow."

Miles began to cry quietly. "You could fight this dad. It isn't like you to give up."

"It's too late mate," Harry paused. He looked apologetic. "You know I was the same with my dad. It's funny how these things come around again. He had the same thing. Well, lung cancer with him. Too many Woodbines." Miles saw his dad look down, recalling the past.

" I was furious with him when he refused to have an operation to remove his lung. He said to me that he was like a car that had gone around the clock. No matter what you fixed something else would go wrong next week. I see now that he was right. I didn't then. I thought that he was a coward. That he couldn't face up to things. It's only now that I understand how brave he was. I've seen enough poor beasts butchered to know that I don't want that."

Harry sat and thought for a moment. "And what I went through with my dad was nothing compared to what happened to your grandmother," he continued. "You remember what she was like don't you?"

Miles nodded. His nan had lived to be 94 but for the last few years of her life she had been suffering from dementia. His mother and father had visited her almost everyday for the last couple of years of her life and he and his brother usually visited every Sunday.

"I've not told you this before, but for the last few months we couldn't take you and Charlie with us when we went to see her," Harry said.

Guiltily, Miles remembered the relief when his parents said that he did not need to come with them to sit in an institutional grey room smelling of cabbage and piss and being asked the same question by his grandmother repeatedly; it was as if a record had got stuck in a groove. He recalled sitting down in the living room with Charlie to watch the Big Match on ITV instead.

Harry continued: "By the end she didn't know who me and your mum was, and she was effing and blinding at everybody, telling me to "fuck off" and calling your mum a slag. I felt sorry for the poor old carers who had to put up with that all day." He paused and then smiled." It must be like sitting in the visitor's end at Millwall."

Miles snorted. He was close to tears and still his dad could make him laugh.

Harry stopped smiling and shook his head. "Anyway, my point is that this isn't as bad as you think it is. I've still got my marbles and I'm in no pain. This bloody stuff is marvellous," he said pointing at the bag of morphine on the stand, which dripped into a tube in his arm.

"Why didn't you tell us before," said Miles sniffing.

"For what purpose mate? So that we can all carry the burden? So that we can all be miserable? It doesn't change the end result does it? Terminal illness destroys families if you let it you know?"

Harry looked thoughtful and was silent for a few seconds. "Your mum has been every day since I have been in here and we've run out of things to say. I hear of people falling in the street with heart attacks or brain haemorrhages. Dead before they hit the floor. Here one minute and gone the next and I think lucky bastards. That way everybody remembers you just as you were. Everybody says it's such a shock but it's a hundred times better than seeing somebody you love rotting away for months or years in front of you. As the Bard said, "It's a consummation devoutly to be wished."

Miles smiled flatly. Harry loved Shakespeare and he recognised the quote from Hamlet. It was a set text for his English O Level and he had memorised all the soliloquies in the play because the teacher said they always came up in the exam. Twenty-five years later he could still remember them precisely. "Where be your gibes now? Your gambols? Your songs? Your flashes of merriment that were wont to set the table on a roar," he quoted.

"Exactly," said his dad. "That's how I want your memories of me to be. But if I'm not careful, this is how you and Charlie will remember me. Some sick old bastard in a hospital bed. Alas, poor Harry. I don't want that," he continued.

Miles sat staring at the floor. He remembered how his dad would take him and Charlie to Millwall. How Harry would meet all his mates in the pie and mash shop and how they had never stopped laughing all afternoon. Having a lark, as his dad would say.

He remembered what he had said when the bully had hit him in the mouth. "Next time, you need to hit him first," Harry had said. "But don't bother punching him." He had shown Miles how to rake with his shoe down his opponent's shin and then keep going so that you stamped straight through onto the bones of the foot. The bully had screamed when he had done that and had to be taken to hospital. But his dad was right, nobody ever touched him or Charlie again. He had worried about getting in trouble with the teachers too. In fact, had been more scared of the consequences than the actual fight. But his dad had been right about that as well. The bully had said nothing. He had told everybody that it happened playing football.

"Have you told mum?" Miles asked softly.

"I will. Tomorrow. I promise. And Charlie, I'll tell him too. Listen, when you come back in, bring a pad and a pen. I need to tell you where everything is. The Will, my pension and bank accounts, things like that," said Harry.

"Dad, you're ill. We can sort it out later," said Miles, taken aback at the practical turn in the conversation.

"No, it can't. I don't want to leave your mum in a mess. The sooner the better."

Miles was crying again. He sat with his head down gulping back the tears. He felt his dad's hand on his shoulder. "Go on son, go home to Kath and my little girl." He always called Evie "my little girl."

Miles put the chair back on the pile. He turned to look at his father. "I love you son," he said. He had never said that before.

"I love you too dad."

Miles had made his way back to his car. He sat hunched with his hands on the steering wheel crying so hard that it made his shoulders shake.

When Miles had finished telling Sharon why Kath had kicked him out she leaned over and held his hand.

"This will all blow over son. I can't think of the amount of times I would have left your father if I'd had anywhere to go. But I would have always come back." She paused. "He left me in the end," she said looking distant. "Stay as long as you want love. You can sleep in your old room." Then she got up to get the fresh bedding out of the airing cupboard.

"Thanks mum," said Miles quietly.

Over the next few months Miles began to rebuild his life. He gave up trying to find a job where references were required. He decided that a job would have to do rather than a career.

After a few weeks working as a barman at a local pub he managed to get a job at Smithfield as a porter. Many people there remembered Harry fondly and were willing to help Miles.

The job meant working from 2am to 10am. This suited him. He was able to look after his mum during the day and occasionally he would travel out to Romford to pick up Evie from school and take her to the park before dropping her off at Kath's.

The situation with his wife was not any better though. She would not let him over the front door step and conversation was perfunctory at best. He supposed that he could not blame her. In her eyes he was a man in meltdown. She was not wrong in reaching that conclusion, but it was not for the reasons she thought. When he thought about too much, which was often, he could not help feeling betrayed.

At weekends he would pick up Evie from Kath's. They would catch the Tube back into London and would visit Borough Market or walk between the food stalls beneath the railway arches at Maltby Street. When they had finished they always went back to his mother's flat in Peckham for tea before beginning the long journey back to Romford.

Miles could not afford a car. Kath had kept the one they used to share. To get to work at Smithfield Charlie had lent him a bicycle. He would cycle through the empty streets of London in the early hours of the morning: up the Old Kent Road, along Southwark Street and across Blackfriars Bridge where he could see the white dome of St. Paul's illuminated in the moonlight.

They were quiet moments. He would peddle along and listen to the tyres whirring below him. On those journeys his mind always replayed the series of events that had led him to this predicament.

In 28 years, he had come full circle: he was back to living in a flat in Peckham with his mother and doing a lowly, unskilled job. Quite often when he arrived at the market people would ask if he had been crying, but he always said that it was the cold wind that blew in his face that was responsible.

One morning late in August Miles cycled home through the sunny city. His mother had gone out. She had an unopened letter for him propped against the salt cellar on the kitchen table. It must have been delivered earlier that morning he thought as he looked at the Romford frank mark on the stamp. He tore open the envelope and unfolded the letter. Kath wanted a divorce.

Chapter 27

It was late in the afternoon when Miles knocked on the door of a small cottage on the outskirts of Cannop Ponds, a small village in Gloucestershire. Brian answered the door and looked warily at the visitor.

"Brian? I don't know if you remember me? You taught me some foraging techniques when I did a Survival Skills course with you last year," said Miles.

"Yes, yes. It's Giles isn't it?" said Brian.

"Miles actually. Sorry to disturb you at home but I have something very important I need to discuss with you. Only you can help me you see?" said Miles, his hands clasped together as if in prayer.

Brian looked nonplussed. "How did you know where I live?" he asked.

"I contacted Outdoor Adventure and told them that I had been on a course with Surety and Guarantee last year and that you had lent me a book on how to identify mushrooms which I wanted to return to you by post. It's a lie I know. I'm sorry but you really are the only person that I can think of who can help me," said Miles with a pleading look in his eye.

"What do you want to talk about?" said Brian furrowing his brow.

"Your exit plan," said Miles

"You had better come in," Brian said opening his front door to let Miles into the cottage.

The two men talked late into the evening and it was only after hearing Miles's full story and gaining an understanding of how desperate he was that Brian eventually agreed to help him.

Miles slept the night on Brian's sofa. In the morning they set off into the forest with a sack, some secateurs and a pair of thick gardening gloves each. Brian found a patch of foxgloves growing in a clearing, the pretty trumpet shaped flowers swishing in the light breeze. Brian looked carefully at one with white flowers. "This is the right one," he nodded donning his gloves and snipping away the leaves that ran down the stem to the base of the plant. He carefully placed them in the sack. "Let's go home," he said.

On returning to the cottage, Brian went straight to the kitchen and tipped the leaves into a pan, poured boiling water from a kettle over them and then left them to simmer for about an hour. He then poured the contents of the pan through a muslin cloth, which lined a sieve.

The liquid dripped slowly into a small bowl. It took a long time. After that Brian used a copper funnel to transfer it into a miniature bottle that had once held gin and then screwed the cap on firmly. The liquid was clear.

"This amount will easily be enough," said Brian. "It will act quickly though so you need to be ready." Miles nodded solemnly. Brian wiped the bottle carefully before handing it to Miles. "I don't want to get the blame for this later on," he said.

"You won't, I promise," Miles smiled sadly.

"It's best taken with alcohol. It speeds up the absorption and will mask any trace of it if a pathologist decides to investigate." He paused. "Well, I had better wash this lot up," said Brian looking at the saucepan, bowl, sieve and funnel. "I don't want the same thing happening to me just yet."

"Thank you," said Miles but the other man had already turned away. "And don't forget to keep paying your life insurance premiums," Brian said over his shoulder.

Miles unlocked the front door of the Peabody flat. "Hello mum, it's just me," he called. He pushed open the door to the living room. His brother, Charlie, sat on the sofa his arms resting on his thighs, his hands clasped together, rocking gently. Miles didn't have to ask to know that his mother was dead.

"Where have you been?" said Charlie hoarsely. His eyes were red and puffy. "I have been trying to call you."

"At a friend's," said Miles. "Sorry, my battery was flat. What happened?"

I came round last night. I rang the bell. No answer, so I let myself in. She was just sitting here. I called an ambulance, but I could see she had been gone for a while. We have to wait for the pathologist's report, but they said that it looked like a heart attack. Actually, a cardiac arrest was what they said, same thing I suppose."

"Where is she now?" Miles asked gently.

"In the morgue at Guy's."

Charlie began to cry softly. "She called me yesterday morning. She said you were away and that she couldn't get hold of you. She was in tears, so I came straight 'round. I thought she was missing dad, you know how she is sometimes? Was," Charlie corrected himself sniffing.

"Oh Charlie, I've been so silly she said. They've had the lot."

"Had what mum? I said.

"All my money, all my savings. It's gone."

" It turns out that some toe rag had phoned her the night before and said he was the police and that someone had cloned her debit and credit cards. He said that he needed to cancel them all and would send somebody to collect them. That she had to write the pin numbers down too. They cleared out her bank account and ran the credit cards up to the max.

"I called the police and they were here most of that morning. They said that this type of thing is very common. They pick on the old and vulnerable. It wasn't much, less than a grand, but she was so ashamed."

Charlie began to sob, his big shoulders moving up and down. "The fucking bastards killed her! For what? For fuck all! A few measly quid. If I ever get my hands on them I'll see that the same thing happens to them," he shouted, his face wet with snot and tears.

Miles sat down next to his brother and hugged him, both crying. Both angry that they had not been here to protect their mother when she had always protected them.

Chapter 28

It was a cold November evening. Miles sat in a café opposite the Café Royal in Regent Street where the Annual Steel Stockholders' Association Dinner was being held. He watched as groups of men dressed in dinner suits and the odd female in an evening dress gave their tickets to a uniformed doorman at the porticoed entrance.

His own dinner suit, dress shirt, bow tie and Oxford shoes were in a suit carrier tucked between his feet. For now, he was dressed in a dark fleece, blue jeans, a leather jacket, trainers and a baseball cap pulled down so that his face could barely be seen.

If he had met somebody who knew him, he doubted that they would recognise him. He had lost over thirty pounds, grown a luxuriant black beard and shaved his head. With the addition of a pair of black thick-framed spectacles he thought that his own mother would not have been able to pick him out of a line-up. Then he remembered that his mother was dead.

Life had got tougher since Sharon had passed away. He missed her. To make things worse he had not been able to pay towards her funeral and Charlie had footed the bill. His brother had said that it was not a problem, but Miles felt ashamed. He promised Charlie that he would pay him back.

Straight after the cremation, he had received a letter from the council saying that it was evicting him from the flat. It had been Sharon's name on the rent book and he had no right to be there, it read. He had gone to the council offices and explained his predicament, but they explained as a single man he was not a priority.

He had ended up renting a single room in a filthy bedsit in Lewisham. Due to his living circumstances, Kath only allowed Miles limited access to Evie now. She had obtained a Court Order stating that his visiting time was restricted to four hours on a Saturday. On his last visit Evie told him that Kath had got a boyfriend and that she was going to get married.

Miles looked up from his coffee and watched as a group of men approached on the other side of the street. They were horsing about and laughing. It looked like they had already been drinking. In the centre of the crowd at the front was Jaimie McGovern. It was the same man he had seen in the wedding photograph and in the bar all those year's ago. He was trimmer and older, but it was the same man. The man who had destroyed his life.

Miles realised then that he had only ever exchanged a handful of sentences with his tormentor. Jaimie McGovern could walk past him in the street and would not know who he was. Miles's downfall was as insignificant to him as brushing a speck of dust from his coat. He had emasculated a man that he was unaware of.

Miles looked at his watch. It was 7.50. He knew he had at least a couple of hours to get prepared. He slowly finished his coffee and then left the café, turned left and started to walk towards Park Lane.

It was a few minutes stroll to the Grosvenor House hotel. Miles pushed through the revolving doors and made his way to the plush toilets by the bar. He locked himself in a toilet cubicle and changed into his evening wear.

He carefully put his jeans and other clothes in the suit carrier and zipped it up. He left the cubicle and checked his appearance in front of the mirror. He had been here before and knew that in this hotel he would not look out of place in a dinner suit. With Christmas parties already taking place it was almost de rigeur.

He set out back to the Café Royale at 9.15. He knew now that the dinner would be finishing, and that people would be preparing to listen to the comedian, guest speaker and long-winded industry bore that they always had at these events.

After checking that there was nothing in the pockets of his discarded clothes, he had left his suit carrier in the toilet cubicle. This must happen in hotels all the time he thought. They will just put it in Lost Property and then eventually throw it away.

Miles arrived at the venue. Already there were small groups standing outside on the pavement smoking. He had not got a ticket, he had no wish to appear on any guest list, but he knew that it was easy enough to latch on to the back of one of the groups of smokers as they re-entered the building. Nobody ever checked your ticket again. Even in the West End it was always possible to get in and see the second half of a play or a concert if you hung around until the interval.

Miles walked up the stairs and studied the table plan in the deserted bar. People were still finishing the wine they had ordered with their dinner. He saw that Jaimie McGovern was on table 8 and walked into the dining room and around the edge of the room until he identified his target.

Somebody at the front of the room tapped a knife on a wine glass and there was an electronic hum before a red-coated Master of Ceremonies said into a microphone. "Ladies and gentlemen, the speeches are about to begin but before we hear from tonight's special guest, Geoff Hurst, and comedian Dave Maddox can we please have a little silence while tonight's sponsor, Alexander Smith-Walker from LBE, gives us a few words."

There followed a light smatter of applause and some shushing. As the speaker rose and all eyes were trained forward, Miles took the white tea towel from his inside pocket and placed it over his right arm. He walked towards table 8 and stopped at the seat occupied by Jaimie McGovern. He leaned down to whisper in his ear "Can I get you some after dinner drinks before the rush starts sir?"

Jaimie nodded. "A brandy for me. Remy Martin. Can you make it a double?"

"Absolutely sir," said Miles writing it down with a pad and pen he had taken from his pocket. He then went around the table taking everybody else's order.

On his way to the bar somebody grabbed Miles by the elbow. It was Bill Thompson. "Can I order a drink please mate?"

"I'm just attending to somebody else, I will come back," he smiled. Bill nodded. No recognition registered in his glazed eyes.

Miles dumped the tea towel on an empty table and made his way towards the bar. He read out the drinks order and had them put on a tray. He ordered a treble brandy for Jaimie McGovern. The bill was an eye-watering £140, which he paid for in cash.

Miles walked away from the bar and placed the tray on a small table. He took the miniature gin bottle from his pocket, unscrewed the cap and poured the contents into the treble brandy. He secured the cap back onto the empty bottle and pocketed it before lifting the tray again and heading for table 8.

Miles went around the table putting a drink in front of each guest. He gave Jaimie his drink last. "They were finishing the bottle so it's a bit larger than a double. I hope you don't mind?" said Miles.

"Fuck off, that's fine," laughed Jaimie. "It's nice to get something for nothing."

"I will leave the tab open in case you want any more?" Miles said quietly.

"Aye, that's fine," said Jaimie lifting the ballooned glass and sniffing its contents.

"It's Mr. McGovern and party isn't it?"

Jaimie nodded. He liked people who were servile.

As Miles made his way down the stairs he could hear the commotion from the dining room. "I think somebody better call a doctor, "he heard the speaker say over the microphone. He exited the building and walked along Regent Street. In the distance, he could see the ambulance picking its way through the London traffic. The reflection of its blue light flashed in the shop windows and its siren wailed. He knew they would be too late.

About the Author

Mike Stott has worked in the Credit Insurance industry in the UK for over 30 years and is currently a broker with Rycroft Associates LLP. He has a degree in Politics and History and lives in the West Midlands with his wife and daughter. This is his first novel.

37026269R00128

Printed in Poland
by Amazon Fulfillment
Poland Sp. z o.o., Wrocław